2089

Written by: Gillian Ellis

Edited by: Caitlin Wahle

For Ana,

Thank you for listening to me read this to you all those years ago

And for Maleah,

Thank you for being my biggest supporter and my best friend

Chapter One:

"We are here today, to count our blessings, and be grateful for the life we have. Even though our circumstances may not be the best…"

David interrupted my prayer. "That's an understatement don't you think Jay?"

"Hush." I opened one eye to scowl at him.

"I'm just saying, we have two impressionable boys here that don't need everything sugar-coated for them." He opened both eyes and turned to our younger brothers.

I kept their hands in mine and continued. "We know that everything happens for a reason, and that You have a plan for us."

David chimed in again. "If he had a plan, why would killing our mother, father, and brother be in it?"

My younger brother's fists clenched mine at the thought of our parents. We all missed them, and our brother Garret too, but David never came to terms with what happened. I kicked him from under the rotten wood table.

"Ouch! The truth hurts doesn't it?" He laughed at my brother's sadness. "I only want them to know the truth. Not whatever you told them."

I opened my eyes and slammed my fist onto the table. "David don't act like you care about anyone else but yourself."

He put a hand over his chest. "Oh, you've hurt me! Ha, you couldn't hurt me even if you tried."

Eddie spoke softly. "Actually, in most fights the two of you have had, Jay has won three fourths of them. So, technically…"

David put his hand over Eddie's mouth. "Shut up nerd! You seem to have an answer for everything, so what's the probability that I'm going to punch you in the face right now?"

I stood up and took Luther's hand in mine. "When you're done being a jerk, come join us while we go find wood."

As I walked through the woods, my thought's surrounded Luther and I.

None of us thought any of this would ever happen. None of the loss that we have gone through, none of the pain, and I certainly never thought that at the age of twenty, I would be parentless, a guardian of my three brothers, and to be known as a criminal in the "law's" eyes.

I remember when the war first started. My family of seven was sitting around the fireplace listening to the news when an amber alert came on. I remember being frightened because it came out of nowhere. I was sitting right by the chair where my father was. I was only fifteen at the time and didn't understand The XYZ Men. Our schools weren't the best at that time; all they wanted to teach us was to keep our mouths shut and do as were told. About twenty minutes into the news broadcast, my parents left the room in a silent manor. I heard them speaking a little bit, but it did not sound positive.

They both came out and called us all to the dining table for a family meeting. We've never had one of those before, so we suspected something was up. We got up from the living room, and walked down the hallway of our four bedroom little cottage we called a home and sat down. Garret was the first to ask what we were thinking, "What's wrong, pop?"

Dad looked over at the cabinet that none of us kids were allowed to touch. The first lesson taught to us was to treat others as we would like to be treated, and the second was to never touch Daddy's cabinet. He opened the door, and it was full from top to bottom with books. Books? What's so dangerous about books? He then took the book labeled, "Hope," pulled it slightly out of the shelf, and then the whole thing swung backward and a dark hole appeared.

"Uh, Daddy, what is that?" my younger brother, Eddie, asked wide-eyed.

"Everyone, come with me," Dad motioned towards the dark hole in the wall. We all sat motionless and expressionless, none of us knew what to think. Well, actually, I take that back. We did know what to think, and it was, what in the world is this cabinet for and what is it doing in our house ?

Garret got up from his seat and moved towards the opening. "Garret what are you doing?"

"Jay, trust dad. He wouldn't hurt us."

I didn't like his response, not one bit. Garret walked up to the opening, and my father reached into the hole, hit the wall, filling the large room with light. Garret went in first. I got up from my chair and stuck my head inside, Inch by inch my head went inside, and more and more of my world crumbled. What else had my parents been keeping from us?

The room had a gigantic map on the front wall with notes all over it. On another wall, there were file cabinets lined up neatly together. On the wall next to it was an entire unit full of weapons. And the fourth wall was packed of non-perishable foods. I go to the grocery store every time with my mother, and I have never seen her get two hundred cans of soup. The secret room was a hideout or something. I turned to dad. He was by the doorway, closing off the opening and locking it with over ten different locks. He turned over to us all, "Now with all of the things happening on the news, you all must know. Your mother and I are part of the Rebellion. It's a mass group of people who are against the ways of our new government. You know that man you've been seeing on the news a lot for the past month?"

I nodded. "Yes, sir."

My father looked over at me. "He is the new leader of The XYZ Men. And he has a plan to take over the world in one swoop. The rebellion has a plan to strike in one week's time, when The XYZ Men is at its weakest point in power. We have only ten thousand men, but the number is growing, and now you all are a part of it."

Luther hadn't been born yet. Eddie was ten, and he understood a little bit. "So we get to shoot the bad guys?" He asked so innocently. I didn't say he was a genius, but I bet that he knew what was going to happen shortly: tragedy and death.

~ ~ ~ ~ ~ ~

"So what's for dinner tonight, Jay?" Eddie put down his hands away from the fire. "We haven't eaten today."

I took my backpack off and opened it. "Well, I could go catch a deer or a bird." I pulled out my bow and arrow. "But it may be too late, wouldn't want to run into a bear."

"Wait, they have bears here?" My little brothers both looked at me with fear filled eyes.

David shook his head, "Nope, we have to make it to across the border now."

I laughed at his statement, "And I wanted to be a lawyer but we can't all get what we want."

He rolled his eyes and turned towards Luther, the youngest of my brothers. "What's your problem?"

Luther remained silent, while turned away from the rest of us. He still hasn't coped with the fact that they are gone. He lost both our mom and dad, and he's not even to double digits yet. I have pity for him.

"Well anyway, Luther, aren't you excited? Your fourth birthday is tomorrow."

David scoffed, "Luther doesn't get excited over anything."

I punched my brother in the shoulder. "Stop picking on him."

David laughed at me. "What, you wanna defend the little ball of depression? Why don't you worry about keeping us alive with food and stuff and leave him to defend himself. That's the only way for him to become a man."

I clenched my teeth, rage spilling out of my ears. I got up off the log and turned to David. "Now you listen here, he is your brother. You shouldn't turn against him or anyone else in this family, or at least what's left of it. I am sick and tired of your stupid attitude, you can either act like you're part of our family or you can leave and fend for yourself like a real man would, if we're using that kinda logic." David got up and walked away, and with him, away went a little part of my sanity.

We woke up the next morning at 4:00 a.m. sharp. I still carried Luther on my back because he needs more than five hours of sleep. David carried Eddie, even though he and Eddie are only two years apart; he's just too lazy to walk before 6:00. We're on our way to the Rebellion's new location since The XYZ Men are onto the old one.

"Jay, aren't we supposed to be there by now? I calculated exactly how long it would take us and we should've been there an hour ago." Eddie pushed up his reading glasses that he had found in a re-location area during a meeting with part of the Rebellion.

"Calm down, all right? I promise we're almost there." I turned around the wall of vines and rocks and I smelled the strong, choking smoke of a fire. The day sky had fallen and it was night. My sense of smell was one of the only senses I could use to our advantage. I signaled to the kids to stop. I waved my hand over to David and pointed towards his machete. I pulled out my rifle, and he came close behind me. I told Eddie to watch Luther and make sure he stays there. Eddie knew what to do.

I heard laughter, and some type of words that I couldn't make sense of. I looked around the rocks and saw about three people. Two were about as tall as David, and one looked like a girl who was not much taller than Eddie. I took a step forward, and so did David.

CRUNCH!

David had stepped on a stick and crushed it to pieces. I panicked, and suddenly one of the tall men came walking cautiously towards us. I gestured for the kids to move further away and to David to be prepared. The man approached us ever so slowly, then rounded the corner quickly like a fox and pounded my back up against the rock.

Chapter Two:

"Who are you?" the man asked me sternly, holding a pocket knife to my throat. David, of course, stood there and did nothing.

"Maybe you should answer that question first." I made one swift move and threw the knife out of his grasp. I elbowed him in the groin and punched him in the face while he was bent over in pain. He fell hard to the ground, and he was out. I gestured for David to put him behind the rock. After we had moved the man, who looked to be about twenty or twenty one, I turned to David and we both knew we had to get the others tied up.

The two others began to shout, "Mark! Mark! Where'd you go buddy?" The other boy came around the corner, and I knocked him out with one swift punch to the face. He flew backwards, and David cracked a smile of approval, like he was proud or something.

"Why can't you do anything to help, huh?"

David rolled his eyes. "Maybe because you never let me do anythin'."

I rolled my eyes towards his pathetic excuse. The younger boy looked to be at least sixteen, a little too young to know not to shout like that in the forest. Otherwise, you might get reported and sent to the LIU.

We tied up the two boys, and I took Eddie and Luther over to talk to the little girl. She had a stuffed animal, which was in the form of an elephant. I took some water from a mud puddle and splashed it onto their faces. The two young men woke up and kept squirming. I took a stick and pointed it into the neck of the one who shoved me up against the wall. "So are you going to answer my question from earlier?"

He laughed. "I thought I had asked you, ma'am." He gave me a smirk, and I was not satisfied with his tone.

"Okay, I'll answer the question. I'm the girl who kicked your butt, and my brothers and I are a part of the Rebellion against The XYZ Men. Now state your business or else."

He laughed and turned to the other one. "Finally."

I was confused. "What?"

"We're part of the Rebellion, too. Don't you remember us from the ceremony for Garret and your father?"

I clenched my teeth. "No, I do not. And you will not speak their names in front of my brothers and I again, got it?"

They both nodded, and the one who pinned me said, "I am Mark, and this is my brother Matthew."

I took the stick away from his face. "Okay, but who is that?" I pointed to the girl.

"That is a little girl we found about two months ago. She was in a town that The XYZ Men had destroyed because they were a part of the Rebellion. We found her hiding in a garbage can in a dump."

I was baffled. "Oh, wow."

Mark laughed, "Now would you be so kind to un-tie us because we need to get moving to the next meeting."

I took the dagger from my pocket and cut the ropes. "Hey, wait! There's another meeting?"

The two brothers nodded. "Yes, and it's just down the road. I would invite you, but you did tie us up and threaten us. Besides, I don't even know your name."

I rolled my eyes. "Wow, you're more of a wimp than I thought, Mark. It only took three moves for a girl to knock you out."

He scoffed, "Fine, you two may come along."

I laughed. "You mean us four."

His eyes widened. "Four? We only have enough room in the vehicle for five people including my brother, the girl, and me. What'll we do with the other three?"

I thought for a second, "Let me see the car." He led me to the old truck hidden under a large tarp.

"If any of the guards knew we had this and we aren't on their side, we'd be sent to the LIU in a split second."

I laughed, "Those guards can kiss my-" I stopped myself from introducing a new colorful vocabulary word to my little brothers; the last thing I need is little boys cursing for no reason. "Butt," I finished.

We stood over the car. We had to devise a plan. "Okay." Mark laid out the map over the hood of truck and pointed at the red starred point right over the border of Ground seven, and then to the red star over some small town. "We're right around the border checkpoint, but luckily the only one we'll have to pass is the one over this ghost town. I will drive and Jay will sit up front alongside me. That way they will think we are a couple. And Matthew and David will sit in the back seat. Since the guards ask too many questions about children, we will hide all three in the bed cooler."

I scoffed and put my hands on my hips. "You think I'm going to let you stick my two little brothers in a cooler? Who knows what you've put in that thing."

He rolled his eyes. "If it helps, I'm putting a little girl that I care about in there also. And I'm only trying to ensure your brothers not being taken and sold by the guardsmen."

I had forgotten about that. For the past year it has been apparent that the guardsmen have been ordered that if any children under the age of fifteen are found, they must be put up for auction. "Oh, right. Sorry." It is an awful thing. Children are the future, and they decide to either auction them off for labor or to just be sent to train until the proper age for being coerced to become a part of

The XYZ Men's work force. They are basically auctioning the future off to not only be diminished, but to never be heard.

We all hopped into the truck and started driving towards the checkpoint. My stomach began to knot in a thousand different places. Mark looked over at me. "What's your problem?"

I peered over at him. "I don't have a problem; I just hope they don't search us."

He laughed and said, "Have a little hope."

We approached the checkpoint, and I put my sunglasses on over my eyes. The guard came up to the window. He had on dark sunglasses and a mustache. He couldn't have been taller than Mark or Matthew, but he looked to be about forty years old. "License and ID, please."

Mark pulled out his wallet and began to dig through the little leather carrier with what looked to be a million pockets. "So how's business been today, sir?" He stood still outside the car and didn't say a word to Mark. "That good, huh? All right, here they are." He handed his two cards to the guard.

The guard looked them over and glanced up at Mark, "Sir, I need you to step out of the car." My stomach dropped. I peered behind me at Matthew. He looked like he was about to faint and was ghostly pale.

"Yes, sir, I will." Mark stepped out of the car and let the man search his pockets; all he found was a gum wrapper. The man let us go, but we were five hours away from our meeting. It seemed like forever, but Mark seemed to be enjoying himself. "I have a question." I kept my head in its same position, facing the car window, enjoying the scenery of nature that hasn't yet been touched. "Jay?" Mark looked at me.

"You were talking to me?"

He nodded, "Who else would I have been talking to? Everyone else is asleep." I looked behind me to see all of them in the backseat leaning on each other's shoulders. It was adorable.

"What do I wanna know?" I asked Mark as he turned sharply, hitting my head on the window. "Ow."

He laughed, "Sorry. I wanted to know what your life story is."

I laughed, "Seriously, you wanna hear that?"

He smirked, "I have to listen to something otherwise I'll fall asleep."

I hit him in his shoulder, "Okay, fine. So when I was little, my father told all of us what was going on with The XYZ Men, and it was pretty scary. I was in school still and studying to become an attorney to help pay for family funds. My family wasn't very wealthy at all. And I trained with my father before he died to defend myself, and now I am working on training my brothers just in case... something happens."

He nodded. "What happened to your mom?"

"Uh, well..." I thought back to what had happened that day. "We all were at a camp site and we had found an abandoned cabin way tucked away in the woods. We had just run out of food for all of us to eat, and Mom had offered to go and refill our packs. Dad wasn't satisfied with that because you aren't supposed to be a woman and out alone without your spouse - you get a fine. She walked out and never returned to us. Dad just told our little brothers that she's in the free land now and we'll see her soon." I began to tear up, but I kept it inside. If you show emotion, you show weakness, and weakness can get you killed.

Mark put his hand over mine, "It is okay to cry you know."

I laughed, "You're funny, and I'm fine." I jerked my hand away.

He turned his head towards me. "We're all going through the same stuff here."

I stopped talking at that point. I was done.

We arrived finally after the long and awkward car ride. The meeting place was an abandoned camp site. No one was there. I looked over at Mark, and he looked very confused. I began to think, What if he is a part of The XYZ Men? What if he was bringing me and my brothers here to kill us off? I got out of the truck and went to go get my younger brothers out of the cooler in the back. I got to the back of the old rickety truck and knocked five times on the cooler and waited for the boys to get out.

Eddie stuck his little head out to see who's outside the cramped space. "Jay! Jay!" He practically threw the lid and leaped out. He squeezed my waist, and I hugged him back.

We started down the side walk, and then I saw a horrid and gruesome scene. There was a field of war, a sea of the Rebellion's members on the ground, either injured or deceased. I motioned for my brother to let the little ones stay behind while Mark, Matthew and I searched for survivors of the brutal attack.

I walked over to a tree and suddenly something grabbed my leg. I screamed, "Mark!"

The man was leaned up against the tree, with one arm completely taken off. He had a gunshot wound to the other arm.

"Ma'am, I have to tell you something. The XYZ Men has asked me to provide you this information." He took a deep and long breath. "Turn yourselves in and take your father's booklets from his lab. You and your family's lives will be spared." The man began to sink down towards the ground.

"Wait, sir! Who told you this?" I grabbed his shirt by the collar.

He sighed, "Jayleen, I cannot tell you. But I will tell you something about your family."

I became intrigued. "What do you know?" I began to tense up, and I screamed, "What do you know?!"

He sunk completely to the dirt. "He's…" He coughed, "He's…"

I screamed once more, "What about my father?!"

The man chocked out one last word: "Alive." His head hit the dirt, and so did my heart.

My father is alive?

Chapter Three:

I began to scream at the man to wake and tell me where my father was.

"Jay!" David approached me cautiously. "Jay, what's the matter?"

My father was alive, so this man said, and I don't even know where to look for him.

"This man just said that Dad is alive and that The XYZ Men wanted me to know it."

David's eyes got wide. "Seriously? This is great news! This means Dad is alive! Why are you upset?"

I turned around and got up. "Because, you idiot, we don't know where he is!"

David backed away, "Okay, there's no need to get angry with me. You're the one who brought us all here to this stupid meeting and nearly scarred our brothers for life. You knew this was shady before we even got in the car, with total strangers I might add. You keep blaming me for all of this but really you should point the finger at yourself." He taunted me by pointing a finger in my direction.

I looked back at the dead man on the ground, then back to my brother. "You think I didn't doubt my decisions before? Do you honestly think that I would try and put you in harm's way? Because if you do, then you're wrong." I walked away towards the truck. We needed to be as far away from there as possible. "Come on, boys! We can't stay here anymore. It is not safe."

"But, Jay, we found a friend!" I turned and looked at my little brothers and they were holding something in a leather pouch, and the pouch was moving.

"What is that?"

Luther shrieked with joy. "It's a puppy! Can we keep it?"

Luther and Eddie both looked at me with wide eyes, "Please?"

I walked over to all my brothers now fawning over the delicate life form. "Guys, I don't know. We already have a strain on food."

"Jay, quit being a buzz kill. Let the children get a puppy," David smirked at me.

We got back into the truck and began to just drive. I looked outside my window, and it began to drizzle little clear droplets of rain on the truck. "There's a storm coming," Mark said looking ahead to the road.

"How would you know? Not like we have the weather man in the car with us."

He laughed, "I can smell it."

I scrunched my nose. "You're weird."

Surely enough it began to storm outside. Mark just laughed and said, "I told you so." As we saw sign by sign go flying by, the car became heavily silent.

I peered over at Mark and he was not looking so good. "Would you like me to drive? You look really tired," I motioned towards the wheel and looked at the side of Mark's head.

"Uh, I don't know," he smiled and looked over at me, "Can you handle it and not crash my baby?"

I laughed, "I am the best driver in my family for your information. But if I drive for you, you have to talk to me while I drive."

He rolled his eyes at me playfully and scoffed, "Fine."

He pulled over, and I got out to go around to the other side of the car. I didn't see the pothole in front of the car. I made one swift stride and next thing I knew, my foot got caught on the edge of the hole. BAM! I was on my face in the cold rain. "Ah!" I screamed as I went down.

"Whoa! What are you doing, Jay?" Matt got out of the truck and helped me get up off of the ground, "You all right?"

I was fairly embarrassed, and I was very mad at myself. "I am swell. I just wanted to enjoy the rain."

He smiled wide and held out his hand for me to grab. I reached for his hand, and he pulled me up, but then he caught his foot in the hole. We both fell, except this time I fell on top of him. It was fairly awkward.

I looked at him and he looked at me, and for a split second we froze. Then, of course, I got back up and apologized to Mark. I had gotten into the car first, and the only thing that was said from the back seat was: "Watch what you're doing, Sis, don't wanna get stabbed in the back by a total stranger."

Chapter Four:

"Jay, I need to go potty," little Luther bellowed.

I smiled, "Okay, you go find David. He'll take you."

"We're here," Mark announced to the boys in the back, "We have to ditch the truck here. Gather your things so we can safely make the transfer. Leave nothing that can lead them to us." I didn't really like this idea of leaving our source of transportation. Call me crazy, but transportation is a necessity during this time.

We've walked about five miles now and nobody's eaten in days. One thing I hate about my brothers is that they insist on being brave and strong and think they can last without eating. I blame David for this behavior.

"You kiddos need to eat something," I said, turning to all the young ones trailing behind me. "Mark and I will go get something. David, you stay with them and supervise."

David scoffed, "Now why do I have to watch the little ones?"

I turned to give him a glare of disapproval. "Because I trust you to keep the kid's safe while Mark and I go find food. You and Matt stay behind. Got it?"

He nodded his head, and once I had turned around, he whispered under his breath, "If I were in charge she'd be staying behind with the truck."

I laughed, "Oh, David, you think you're so funny."

David gets closer to me. "That's because I am, Jay." I could smell his bad breath from a mile away, but up close it'd make your eyelashes fall out.

"Well, David, anything else you wanna tell me?"

He cleared his throat slowly, as if taunting me to ask him again. "I hate this situation we're in. We're in who knows where, and on top of that, we're with three total strangers that you just let walk into our journey. Hey, we don't even know if these idiots are a part of the Rebellion or not! Wake up, Jay, it's kill or be killed now; it's survival mode time."

I chuckled, "You know what, everyone, listen up. You all have a choice in life: to be positive or to be negative. Now, I know how our situation is at the moment. But find the positive in every situation you face, and your life will reflect your positive thinking. Now you can choose to be a sourpuss your whole life, that's fine by me," I point and wave my finger vigorously at David, "But I will choose to be kind towards others and protect what's near and dear to me at all costs."

Of course David had his normal response, to roll his eyes at me and walk away. I honestly didn't care, because I saw the way my other brothers were thinking through their facial expressions, and I knew that I got through to someone.

"Jay, it's getting late. I think we should stay here and set up camp," Matt said. That was the first time I've heard him make a noise since we first met. I looked towards the sky; it didn't even look dark or relatively darker than it was just a minute ago. I agreed and we set up the tarp and blankets under a large tree.

"So, why don't we all share something about ourselves, shall we?"

I gave David an annoyed look, and he is already smirking in approval of his action. He doesn't care about learning new things; he just wanted to find something I say or Mark or Matt say and twist it into something entirely different. I was not looking forward to the arguing.

And then David bellowed, "Why don't we start with you?" David pointed towards Mark.

Mark politely smiled at David, "Hm… something about me." He paused. "Something about me is I don't like people who are inconsiderate towards their family. Just something I thought you all should know." Mark looked right at David afterward, and David looked furious.

"You listen here, buddy," he pushed Mark, "you better watch yourself. Because I can beat your…"

"Stop, before you embarrass yourself in front of your brothers by trying to talk like you have an education. And, also, I am not your 'buddy.' I am someone who is helping you, and if you don't appreciate that I suggest you leave."

David backed away, and went into his own tent he had set up and closed the tarp behind him.

Mark walked over to me and sat on the log next to the fire, to my left. "Look, Jay, I am sorry about having to talk to your brother like that, but it is very disrespectful towards you and is an abominable example of behavior for your brothers. I had to call him out for it. Plus, it's hilarious when he tries to be all that."

I laughed, "Oh, it's all right. I know he needs it." But actually, it kind of bothered me. *How could Mark flip just like that?* So calm one moment, then the next completely different. I realize David was out of line, but it was a bit much.

He suddenly slipped his hand behind my waist and pulled me closer to him. My eyes widened and I pulled away. "What are you doing?"

He grinned devilishly. "Just keeping you warm."

I rolled my eyes and pushed him away. "I'm plenty warm thank you." *That was awkward.*

Mark and I were still sitting by the fire, having talked for another two hours, when suddenly I heard a gunshot. It was followed by a second, and then a third. And with the third gunshot, I screamed in pain as the bullet penetrated my leg. I fell to the ground and blacked out.

I saw split visions of the things occurring around me. The first time I got a glimpse of what looked like men with large rifles. Then I heard them rustling through the tents and breaking equipment. I also heard the men talking and one said, "There were more, but we only have the girl and the boy."

Another asked, "Should we go look for the others?"

"No, we have the one Mr. X requested and one casualty; we don't need more."

And that's when I knew that that might be the day I die.

Chapter Five:

I was greeted by the sound of a steady beep. It was repetitive, sounding every three seconds. It was bright, and I had to squint my eyes to keep it from blinding me.

There was a brutally beaten man next to me. He was fairly tall and had dark hair. His face was covered with blood, and it looked as if he had been shot in the lower abdomen. I looked down at his shoes and realized who the man was: Mark. I looked towards his vital sign reader; he was stable.

"Mark," I whispered.

He didn't move.

"Mark!" I said a little louder than I liked.

He still didn't move.

"MARK!"

"SHHH," he exclaimed, "Jay, would you like to get us killed?"

"You're alive?!"

He nodded, "Yes, I am. Now I hope you know where we are."

I looked around. "A hospital?"

He tried to turn towards me, but his injury prohibited him to not do so, "We're in the LIU."

I thrashed and struggled, but stopped because my leg began to throb. I tried to pull my arm up, but it was strapped to the hospital bed. I edged the blanket off my leg and saw how badly bruised it was and all the bandages that went along with it.

I gasped, "What happened to my leg?!"

Mark sighed, "That night, when they ambushed us, they greeted us with gunfire." Mark coughed aloud in the middle of his sentence. "One of the men shot you in the leg. You underwent surgery about two days ago. I suggest that you quit thrashing around."

I was angry and confused. "I don't know what to do, and we may die in here."

~ ~ ~ ~ ~ ~

It'd been a week, and I hadn't moved a muscle. Every once and a while Mark would be assisted by a nurse to take a walk around the hospital.

I turned to Mark, who was sitting up now. "Hey, Mark. Why would they kidnap us, chain us to a hospital bed, but keep us alive and heal us?"

He looked off into the ceiling, "I heard them talking."

I tried to lift up my head. "Are you going to tell me what you heard?"

He rotated his head, "I shouldn't shake you up right now."

I shook my head, "No, it'll make me get shook up if you don't tell me what they said, now spill it Mark."

He chuckled, "You're cute when you're demanding."

I got up that time. "What?"

"What..." he said, confused by his own statement.

I changed the subject quickly to avoid awkwardness. "Tell me what they said."

"The minors are ready for transport now," one of the nurses said while talking to two guardsmen.

Suddenly, I felt a sharp pain in my arm. Everything went black, but I could still hear.

Mark put up a fight, so they had to gather up more nurses to hold him down to give him the same shot I received. I heard one of the guardsmen say something frightening. "Bring them to The XYZ Men's center for holding. Mr. X has been waiting for a very long time for this; don't lose these two."

Chapter Six:

I woke up in a dark and damp place. I squirmed to get up, but my hands were tied behind me in a metal chair. I no longer had a hospital robe on, but now I had my old clothes. Strangely they were clean and stainless. I looked to my left. Mark was there.

Suddenly, bright blue lights turned on. They were blinding, and I jumped because it scared me. I looked up and saw four guards come in through a metal door. I realized that Mark and I were in an interrogation room.

The four guardsmen were heavily armed. One of the men's radio devices beeped, and a voice came over it, "He's there. Open the door to grant access." That same man went to the door and pressed a bunch of buttons and the door slowly unlocked and opened.

A tall old man walked into the room, in a fancy suit. He smiled creepy, had a British accent, and was exaggeratedly tall. So he was your typical super villain type person. He smiled creepily, "Do you know who I am?"

I shook my head, "No."

He chuckled, "Oh, dear, sure you do. Think a little harder Miss Tane."

I glanced over at Mark, he looked frightened. "Let us go," I looked into the man's eyes, and they were as black as his soul.

"Young lady, I have been waiting four years for this moment, and you think I am just going to let you go? Ha. No, no." He grinned devilishly, "I have plans for you Miss Tane. Your father was useless to me. I need you to tell me where the cellar is." He began to step closer.

"What cellar?" I looked over at Mark; he still had the same pale and emotionless look on his face.

"Oh, Miss Tane, is this young man yours?" The tall man walked towards one of the guardsmen and whispered into his ear. The guard walked behind Mark and shocked him with some device. He yelled in pain.

"Stop it!" I shouted.

The man laughed, "This is a grand time. Yes?" He grinned at me, "We took you in, and fed you, and healed you, and *this* is the thanks you give me?"

I sat up, "Why are you torturing him? He did nothing wrong, release him and just keep me instead. Release him!"

The man laughed again. "You see, Miss Tane, I don't take orders from others; I give them. The reason I cannot let your little man friend go is because he is involved in my plan. Besides, why would I harm you physically when I can harm what you love?" He gave me another devilish grin. "He reminds me of your father; he screamed the same way before he died."

I began to scream, "You're sick!"

He snickered "Hear that wonderful sound? Sweetie, do you even know the difference between being mad and being crazy?"

Suddenly, the man threw his fist at my right cheek, landing a punch. My lip began to bleed. He shook his hand in the air.

"The difference between being mad and crazy is that you only become mad, but you are born crazy."

I spit on his shoes. "You're worse than mad; you're the meaning of evil."

The man smiled, "You're too kind, Miss Tane, again too kind. But, young lady, didn't that criminal of a mother of yours ever teach you manners?"

I spit again, the taste of blood trickled in my mouth. "Yes, she did, but she also told me never to speak to strange old men, yet here I am talking to you."

He laughed. "Young lady, I am not a strange old man. In fact, I am not a man at all. I am a fragment of your imagination, I am nowhere on the grid. If you tell anyone of my existence, they will simply not know what or who you are talking about, because I am not a man. I am a force not to be reckoned with, though, Miss Tane, don't doubt that."

He started towards Mark. "Now, young sir, what is your name?"

Mark opened his mouth to speak, but the man stopped him.

"Don't even think about lying to me, Mr. Holloway, since I already know everything about you." The old man picked up a thick file and opened it. "Now, your full name is Mark Christopher Holloway, you have a younger brother, and you've been in and out of Juvenile Prison for petty crimes. And you were born you were born here. Oh, my!"

The man began to laugh as he slowly walked towards the door. Before he left he turned to me, "Your lover's father is Dr. Z. Also the man who killed your mother." The man slammed the metal door, and I could feel my face turn red in anger.

~ ~ ~ ~ ~ ~

"How could you have not told me that your father is... one of them?" I glared at Mark, his head was down.

"I am sorry, Jay, but I knew if I were to have told you that you never would've trusted me or my brother. I truly am sorry."

I stared at him with anger spilling through my veins. "Whatever."

Mark laughed, "Jay, I absolutely hate my father. You think I joined the Rebellion because I like him and what he's doing to innocent people?"

"Mark, I don't care about what your father did, or that he is probably the one who killed my mom, but that you never even had the courage to tell me to my face. I had to hear it from a guy who kidnapped us from the woods!"

Mark met my gaze finally, "That man is Mr. Y, the assistant leader of the XYZ men."

The door was knocked upon, and one of the guards opened it. Mr. Y walked inside, "Well, Mr. Holloway, your father has been informed of your wellbeing and said that he is excited to come and visit you! Isn't that just marvelous?"

Mark looked at the man, and looked back down at his tethered feet.

Mr. Y spoke again, "But your father did have one request," he paused, "Your father would like your brother to join you, so we have sent out search parties around the area in which we captured you. You all will be reunited once more!"

Mark scuffed his shoe on the ground. "I don't want to see him."

Mr. Y turned to Mark. "Excuse me?"

"Are you already losing your hearing, sir? I said I don't want to see my father." Mark looked over at me and smiled. *Why is he smiling at a time like this?*

Mr. Y got a chair from across the room and slowly dragged it to sit in between Mark and me. "You know, Mr. Holloway, we can find your brother as your father wished, or we can find him brutally murdered with the rest of your little group in the woods. It's your choice, Mr. Holloway."

Mark laughed. "Sir, treat me however you want, and do to me as you please. But we have a rebellion behind us that is twice the size of your army. And the one thing we have and you don't is motivation. You may have taken away our freedom and our happiness in life, but we will insure that you do that to anyone else after us."

We'd been in that place seemingly forever. There weren't any windows or clocks visible. I began to weaken; they hadn't given us anything except dirty water, which I barely drank. I had been sitting in that chair, in the same position forever, and the only thing running through my mind is if my brothers are all right. That's the only thing I was worried about, my brothers.

Chapter Seven:

"Hello, Maggots! Time for transport." Mr. Y walked in and stomped his overly expensive boot on the concrete floor. Two guards came and untied Mark from his chair, and then chained his hands behind his back. These chains weren't just any chains. These were the electric shocking chains, and if you move and squirm too much, they automatically go off.

Another set of guards came back later and untied me, but they didn't put the chains on me. They put these bizarre cuff like objects around my wrists. They picked me up from my chair and brought me down a dark, metal hallway. I realized by the look of where we were that we were still in the United States, but I didn't know in which region. Around 2078 they officially took away voting rights from all citizens, even the rich people. They believed that we needed three people that "knew what they were doing" to rule all humanity. They took away the governments from other countries and started calling all the continents Pangea again to "avoid confusion," as they said. I just think they were too lazy to try and remember the countries they ruled.

"Get up," the guard commanded. I slowly got up from the old wooden bench they made me wait for what seemed to be half an hour. They took me again down a long never-ending hallway to a vault door of some sort. One guard pushed me over to the other guard and punched in a bunch of numbers into a keypad and even scanned his thumb print afterward.

The vault door opened, and I was blinded; it was actual sunlight. I hadn't seen it in what seems like forever. A sudden gust of wind entered my nostrils: fresh air. But then the air became different: it smelled of the sea.

I squinted my eyes, attempting to lessen the light that was currently blinding me. I took a look over at the guard to my left; he was wearing a fairly clean uniform and didn't seem very talkative.

But the guard on my right was wearing a bright pink bracelet, which looked as if his daughter had made it special, just for him. "So, how old is she?"

"I beg your pardon?" The guard still looked ahead.

"How old is your daughter? I saw your bracelet and assumed…"

The guard looked over at me. "She died a long time ago along with her mother." He looked away and tucked the bracelet under his white uniform sleeve.

"I'm sorry for your loss, sir. You know I have lost family, too."

"Haven't we all, kid? Listen here, keep your mouth shut and listen whenever you're on the boat. You learn things when you listen and don't speak."

I nodded. "If it means anything, she's looking down at you proudly right now."

The guard laughed. "Ha, no, she wouldn't. I'm working for the XYZ Men, hurting innocent people. She's not proud, probably disappointed."

I shuffled my feet across the dock, "No, sir, you're living for her. You aren't the XYZ Men, you aren't hurting innocent people." The man kept his same position, standing straight and looking forward.

"Look, little lady, we don't have much time until we have to go aboard the ship and I have to leave you. Listen and listen well. They plan to attack against the Rebellion in eight days' time, but it's where they're taking you. They plan to execute you there, to show others involved in the Rebellion what happens when you disobey the XYZ Men. I suggest you inform the head of the Rebellion soon or else we have no hope. You're our only hope for freedom."

I nodded. "Thank you, sir."

Three differently dressed guards came to us from the boat and jerked me away. They walked me to the steps. "Get up there, princess, we don't have all day." I walked up the steps and never said a word.

"Name?" The clerk at the desk in the prisoner wing of the ship asked me.

"Jay Tane." I scuffed my shoe on the ship floor.

"Full name?"

I sighed heavily, "Jayleen Rick Tane."

"Your cell number is 4298; go get your uniform and shoes and meet in the mess hall. You'll get instruction for transport soon."

I walked down the poorly lit hallway towards my cell. Each number went by, harder to remember than the last: 4289, 4290, 4291, 4292, 4293. In cell number 4294 there was Mark and some other man on the bottom bunk bed. "Mark!"

Mark jumped up and ran to the cell door, "Jay! What are you doing here?"

"I have no earthly clue, but I have something to tell you. The guard told me they plan to attack the Rebellion in eight days' time. We have to warn the Rebellion before it's too late!"

"Hey, Prisoner!" a guard yelled from down the hall, sprinting towards me. Suddenly, the giant, 200 pound man tackled me and put me in hand cuffs.

"Ow! Get off me," I shouted. Mark just stood there, on the other side of the cell wall and didn't say a word. I looked up to see if Mark was there, and he was. He just stood there, staring at me, not doing a single thing.

Chapter Eight:

I put on the hideous navy blue jumpsuit and terribly stiff black shoes. Then came in a girl that looked to be a little younger than me.

"So you're the fresh meat, huh?"

"Excuse me, and who might you be?" I looked at the girl, startled.

"Oh, excuse my manners. Guinevere Charles, and who are you?" The girl had a British accent, long red hair, and spoke soft.

"I'm Jay Tane."

The girl gasped, "Jayleen Tane? Oh my! You're here! The Rebellion in our parts has only heard stories of you and your family saving us, but now I know you're real! What is your plan to get the XYZ Men out of power?"

I was very overwhelmed. "Uh…"

The girl laughed, "Oh, sorry. I probably shouldn't be speaking so loudly." She lowered her voice to a whisper, "Are you here to spy?"

I sighed. "Um, Guinevere, is it?"

She laughed. "Nobody has called me that in forever. People just call me Gwen."

I nodded. "Ok, Gwen. I am not here to spy. I was captured about three weeks ago by the XYZ Men with my friend Mark. I have no plan, but I am developing one right now."

Gwen just looked at me wide eyed. "So you have no plan to help us all?"

I smiled, "Don't worry, Gwen, this war will be over soon."

Gwen smiled back, but was tearing up. "What's wrong, Gwen?" I put my hand on her shoulder.

"Well, you're right about the whole 'it'll be over soon' part. I'm scheduled a one way ticket to the LIU in three days." Gwen began to cry.

"Oh Gwen, I'm so sorry."

She wiped away her tears with her hoodie sleeve. "Oh, its fine. Not like I have anything else to do. I already have a life sentence for auto theft, and now it's just three days until I go home." Gwen smiled again. "It's like my mum always told me, 'Guinevere, if you don't belong somewhere, find another place. There's a place for everyone in this world, you'll find yours someday.' I believe that my place isn't where I am not free."

I sighed. "I promise you, Gwen, before I leave this earth, we will all be free from the XYZ Men's reign of terror, and that's a promise I am never going to break."

Gwen wiped away the tears once more. "Thank you, Jayleen, it really means a lot to everyone."

I smiled at her, and gave my new friend a hug. I knew I needed to save Gwen from dying in the LIU.

"Jayleen Rick Tane?" a guard bellowed from down the hallway.

I stuck my hand through the bars on the cell door, "Here."

The guard slowly walked down the way towards my cell. He arrived at the cell and unlocked the door. "Miss Tane, your transport is about to begin. Please put these on and meet us in the transport chamber; that's room 5029."

I slowly took off the jumpsuit from the first day I got here, and put on the tight elastic jumpsuit they gave me. It almost seemed like a diving suit. It was awkward, because the guard stood at the door while I changed.

Before I left I turned to Gwen. "May you be free in the near future." I hugged her, and she held onto me tightly.

"And may you save the world in the near future." She smiled at me, holding back her tears. I took a deep breath.

"Stay strong for me, please," Gwen said as I walked out. "I will if you do the same for me."

I walked down the hall to the room the guard indicated, hearing a crowd of some sort. A roar of cheers bellowed along the halls of the ship. I got to room 5029, and the roars and cheering were ear bursting loud now.

There were two guards at the front doors. "Name?"

I sighed, "Jayleen Rick Tane." I was honestly sick and tired of the asking of my full name at this point.

"Once you go in, please wait until the buzzer sounds and walk through the double doors across the room. Do you understand the instructions I have given you, Jayleen Tane?"

"Yes, sir."

I walked into the room and sat in the chair by the double doors. The room had mostly darker colors splashed throughout. I started to get nervous. I didn't know what was behind that door. What if it was my family all in a room, and I had to watch them die? What if it was Mark being slowly killed in front of me? The possibilities for the XYZ Men to torture me are endless, and that was horrifying.

Suddenly the alarm went off, a red light appeared over the doors, and they opened automatically. It was hot and bright on the other side of the doors, and the crowd began to howl. *What was going on?*

~ ~ ~ ~ ~ ~

I took three steps, each step harder than the last. I began to sweat, it was super-hot out. Maybe it was nerves, but then I saw the crowd. They were sweaty, too.

I was in an arena. There were tall walls all around me and only two entrances. I looked around the crowd, and it had a large majority of wealthy people. I over looked the arena and found the XYZ Men booth, on the highest floor, with the most elegant setting, of course. There was Mr. Y, smiling creepily down at me. Then the crowd roared once more as a young man entered the arena.

A speaker crackled above, "Welcome, world's Sergeants, world's leaders, and the XYZ Men. Today, we will witness Jayleen Rick Tane, the daughter of the man who organized the Revolution, versus Mark Christopher Holloway, the son of our beloved Dr. Z. Now, place your bets. Once the timer goes off, the battle for life will begin. Warriors, approach your marks in the middle of the battle ground."

I walked slowly over to the line where I was supposed to stand.

"Mark, can you believe they're doing this?" He laughed at me. "I'm sorry, is something funny?"

He laughed again, "Oh, you naïve girl, you."

I was puzzled. "Mark?"

He laughed harder. "Oh, please, don't make killing you harder than it needs to be. Did you seriously think that I would be part of the Revolution if my father is Dr. Z? Ha, Jay." He tried to touch my face but I jerked away.

I looked at him, but couldn't find words to spit out.

"Jay, you honestly thought that you could find true love with stranger that you found in the woods? I expected more from you, especially considering who your father was."

I opened my mouth to speak, "I-."

"That's just what I had expected from you: nothing. Ah, I cannot wait for this to be over so I can go find my brother and tell him we don't have to pretend anymore. In advance, I'm sorry for your loss. The little ones I'll miss, but David not so much."

I wiped away the sweat on my brow. "Go ahead, keep talking."

He laughed at me and threw his hands up. "Oooo, I'm so scared, you're acting tough now." The pedestals rose from the ground with two machetes. Mark and I both grabbed a weapon and kept it close.

I still cannot believe it. Mark turned out to be the bad guy. He was so nice to me, though. I guess some people have a way of hiding things from others, but David saw it. Maybe I was just blinded by what could've been. But in this world you never know a person's true self. And now I know for sure: trust no one.

Suddenly, the timer went off, and Mark and I got into our positions. The speaker crackled on once more, "Let the battle begin."

Chapter Nine:

I kept my head facing forward, never taking my eyes off Mark, who was dead to me.

The battle for my life had already begun. I just stood there, waiting for Mark to make the first move. But he just stood there. I lunged forward, and the blade of my machete glided across his arm. But he lunged forward and sliced my leg down the back, "Ah!" I cried in pain, but he remained emotionless.

He jumped forward again and stabbed my other leg. I clenched my teeth as I fell to the ground, "Oh!" I cried out as I hit the earth.

"So, Jay." He squatted to become level with me, "When did you think this was going to end up in your favor, huh? You're real stupid, you know, to think a stranger in the woods would become your best friend. Did you have feelings for me or something? Because that's the only reason I can think of for you to trust me so quickly." He laughed at me.

I had a flood of memories rush through my head. The first one was of my whole family picnicking in our backyard. I was only seven at the time, and most of my brothers were either babies or not even born yet. We had no idea of what was happening around us in the world then; there wasn't the XYZ Men or a Revolution.

The next memory I saw was when I got a letter the day before my father and brother disappeared. It read,

Dear beloved Jay,

Things will begin to change for you very soon. If for any reason your brother and I die out there tomorrow, please take care of your brothers for me. I know your mother would be so proud of the woman you have become, as am I. I have known you will do great things. Remember your strength is stronger than any other person's power.

Love, Dad

I opened my eyes. Mark was just sitting there, watching me. He took his blade and pushed it slowly into the leg he had already cut. I cringed as the blade went deeper and deeper into my flesh. He twisted the blade, slicing my flesh more and more. I began to cry silently. Then I remembered what my father had told me, "Remember your strength is stronger than any other person's power."

I looked over at Mark. He turned away from me to look at the highest level, and then I struck him with a swift kick to the side. I got up off the ground and took his weapon from him. I pointed it at his face. "You can never have feelings for something that isn't real." The crowd had stopped cheering and become silent. Mark got up slowly. "You realize that this will only end one way: with you dead. Even if you kill me, they'll kill you after. There's no point in fighting the XYZ Men, Jay. You'll never win. Let me put you out of your sweet misery."

He swung at me and took his weapon back. He leaned backward, and then charged me. I ran towards him, screaming. I pulled my machete out and pointed it at his center mass.

As we approached each other rapidly he screamed at me, "You'll never win Jay!" His face was covered in blood, and so were his clothes. He finally made contact with my machete, and I stabbed him through the chest. I dropped my machete in disbelief of what I had done. He began to cough rapidly, and coughed up a little blood.

I turned to look for my weapon, and I felt a sharp pain in my arm. I looked to see a gunshot wound. I shouted at the highest level, "That's not a fair fight! He gets a gun!" Suddenly, Mark tackled me from behind. I fell and scraped my chin on the dirt.

He pinned my arms down and began to repeatedly punch me in the face. I spit at him, and he continued. I finally stopped moving. I began to black out, all I could hear was cheering, and Mark's laughter. I began to talk to myself. *You can't die like this.*

He again let his ego get the best of him, as he paraded himself around the arena. He picked my limp body up off the earth and put me over his shoulder. He began to show me to the crowd, shouting, "See? I told her she couldn't win!!" I looked down and noticed the outline of a knife in Mark's back pocket. I slowly reached for it, and stabbed him in the back. He fell upon his knees.

I fell to the ground. I got up slowly and walked towards him, who was now cowering.

I cracked a crooked smile of my own, "I will win, dead or alive. I have the Revolution on my side, you know. All you have is power lust."

I took my machete and turned it around so that the handle was facing Mark, and then I hit him across the face with it.

He thumped onto the dirt.

I then took my weapon and stabbed him once more in the abdomen. I turned around to the top level and glared at them. Mr. Y smiled devilishly at me and applauded.

They all got what they wanted. I participated in an unruly act and killed a boy. A boy whose young, impressionable mind was sculpted and molded to a form of darkness. I gave in to the madness. I gave in to the evil nature of these people.

Two guards came into the arena and took me by the arms. They dragged me to a dark, cold room. The guards threw me backwards to the floor, walked out of the room, and slammed the door shut. I scrambled to get up, but my leg gave out on me.

A man walked into the dungeon. He appeared to be tall, and it wasn't Mr. Y. They kept the lights off as he walked in and shut the door behind him. It was pitch black, and I couldn't see anything. I was scared for my life. *Is this man a man they hired to execute me?*

"I know what you're thinking," the man whispered under his breath. "But I am not here to harm you in any way, Jayleen." I scooted back against the wall in an attempt to get away from the man. "But I need your help, Jayleen. If you help me, I will set you free. The XYZ Men will leave you and your family alone forever."

I laughed, "You don't want to help me, and I certainly don't want to help you."

I felt something brush up against me. "But, Jayleen, you mustn't pass up the opportunity that is upon you." He paused, and I felt hot air in my ear. "If you tell me where the Rebellion Cellar is, then I will set you free." He pulled something out of his pocket. I cringed, thinking of all the different weapons he could use on me.

A small light erupted from his fingertips, and then sustained itself on the end of a cigarette. He shoved a cigarette between his teeth and took its smoke into his lungs. He then walked towards me. He squatted, and then blew a rush of smoke into my face.

I coughed, "Those can kill you, you know."

"We're all going to die someday anyway. Now tell me where the Cellar is."

You see, the Cellar was our old house from my childhood. The Cellar kept all of my father's important items of business and secrets.

I kept thinking of the scenarios, all the good and bad outcomes. I knew that I needed to tell the mystery man where the Rebellion Cellar was before I died there, in that rotting cell. "Okay, sir, I will tell you where it is, but you must do me a favor."

"My ears are open Miss Tane," the man stood there silently.

"If I tell you where the Cellar is, I must be able to bring a friend."

He laughed at my request, "You want to bring the boy who tried to kill you? He's dead. You're more stupid than I thought dear."

I smiled through the blood on my teeth from my busted lip, "He's not the friend I had in mind."

Chapter Ten:

On the plane, it only took a few hours to get to our destination. My palms were sweaty with excitement, and nerves. I wanted to get home, and find my family.

"This is where you would like to be dropped off, correct, Miss Tane?"

I nodded, "Yes, sir."

The aircraft dropped down to the ground gradually, and once it landed I jumped off of the air craft and turned around to the guardsmen. I was surprised because the man had broken the Guardsman code by smiling at me as if he had known me. Then I noticed something very vibrant on his wrist, and it was pink. I ran back towards the aircraft to say hello to the man, but they had already taken off.

We began walking. They had dropped us off in what used to be the United States of America, 74 years ago. We passed a broken and rusted sign that read, "Welcome to Texas. Drive friendly – The Texas way!" Yeah, right, like I will be doing any driving anytime soon.

"So, Jayleen, where are we going to find your family?"

"Now, Gwen, you can call me Jay, remember?" Gwen smiled.

"Again, Jay, thank you so much for saving me, I owe you my life," she giggled with joy.

"It's nothing Gwen, you don't owe me anything. I had made a promise, and I wasn't going to break it."

We had little time to find my family and get to the Rebellion headquarters in the U.S. before the XYZ Men figure out that I gave them the address to an old grocery store we once stopped at while on vacation two continents away. I believed we had a week until they tracked us down.

"Hold on, can we please take a break?" I put my hand on the tree next to me so that I could keep my balance, "Ever since the battle in the arena I haven't been able to travel very far for long amounts of time you know?"

She nodded, "Jay, take all the time you need." She walked over to a deserted barn and shook the doors, but they didn't budge. Gwen, who was about five feet, took a step back and paused. She charged the door and cracked the old barn wide open. Gwen turned to me and shouted, "Jay, would you like to stay here tonight? I think it'll be good for your legs to rest indoors!" I nodded and got up off the dirt.

I strolled up to the barn and the giant doors creaked whenever you touched them. I took one step into the barn; it was pitch black. I stumbled around to find something to hold onto, but I couldn't. All of a sudden, the old barn was given a second chance at life. The lights burned bright in their former glory. I looked to my side, and there was a giant ladder that led to an overhang above me. I proceeded to get to know the barn.

"Gwen," I whispered, "where are you?" I heard her giggle aloud, and then I saw her pop her head over the other overhang across the barn. "There you are! Want me to come over there?"

She smiled. "No, thanks, but I know we are staying here tonight."

I laughed, "Okay, so what was your family like Gwen?"

She became silent for a moment. "Well, I was born in the United Kingdom, and I am from a fairly strict English family. I was named after a great grandmother or something, and they all support the XYZ Men only because they have the money to keep themselves safe. But, we secretly support the Rebellion. My parent's weren't happy about it at first, but once they took my little sister, they came around."

"Oh, wow, and I hope you don't mind me asking... but how'd you end up in the processing center?" She was silent again, as if she was debating telling me or not. "Gwen, I will not judge you because of it, we all have a past."

Gwen smiled. "Okay, well, I was on my way to the U.S., that was where all the fighting was at the time, and I stopped in a deserted town similar to this one. Well... a man decided to kidnap me in my sleep and keep me for a servant of some sort."

I gasped quietly. "Oh, my."

She nodded, "Yeah, so after being held against my will for a few weeks, I killed him in his sleep so he couldn't hurt me." Her voice became shaky. "Every day I think back to that moment and ask myself if it was worth it. I still haven't given myself a valid answer, you know." She sighed. "I can still hear the sound of his last breath escaping his mouth. It's the scariest thing you can hear."

"Gwen, if there's one thing I know about, it is regrets. You have a choice in whether to reflect on every horrible moment in your life, reliving them over and over again, or you can choose to simply learn from both the bad and the good experiences in your life, and move on."

She smiled looking at me longingly. "If I wasn't so tired, I'd come across this barn and hug you right now!"

We both laughed, and I climbed up the ladder to sleep on the top level of the barn. As I looked out of the cracks of the wood at the sunset, Gwen went back down to the main floor. I sat on a large bale of hay, and watched as the sun went down. I smiled, it was so beautiful. I laid down and fell asleep. It was nice to go to sleep knowing I was safe.

~~~~~~

I woke up to the sound of loud talking. I rubbed my eyes to try and wake myself up. "Gwen," I squeaked while pushing a morning yawn out. I rolled over to look beyond the ledge for Gwen, but she wasn't in her bed or on the barn floor. Regretting even getting up because I was so comfortable, I rose and headed cautiously down the ladder. I moved the barn door slightly to look outside, and witnessed Gwen being choked by a young woman. "Gwen!" I ran towards her and shoved Gwen out of the woman's grasp. "State your business, and it better be good!"

"Jay!" Gwen shouted, "Let her go! She's a friend!"

I looked at Gwen's terrified expression, then below at the stranger who I had put into a headlock. "Oh."

I released the woman, and she just stood there blankly staring at me. "So who are you?" I put out my hand for her to shake, but she just kept staring at me.

Gwen came up behind her and put a hand on her shoulder. "This is Ellie, and she's mute." Ellie smiled and waved at me. I waved back.

"I've never met a mute person before. Can she hear me?"

Gwen laughed, and so did Ellie. "Yes, she can hear you. She just cannot speak."

I nodded. "Oh, my bad, Ellie."

They both smiled. "I met Ellie at this underground club for Rebellion members only, it's kept secret though."

I looked at them in disbelief, "Club Nine is real?"

Gwen laughed, "Yes! Ellie manages it and has invited us over to stay! Shall you join us?"

"Uh, I don't know, it feels like a storm is coming. Should we really be out in these conditions?"

Ellie shook her head rapidly and poked Gwen in the shoulder, like Gwen had forgotten something. "Ah, yes! It's underground, you know, very safe. And only ten minutes away." Gwen smiled as if she desperately wanted to go. I looked up at the sky, knowing it was going to storm badly soon, and we needed a better shelter than an old barn that could fall apart any minute.

"We'd better get going if we are going to get there before the storm hits."

They both jumped with excitement. "Thank you so much, Jay," Gwen and her friend began to walk away, but turned and gestured me to follow them.

We had walked down a dirt road to an old gas station with boarded up windows. Ellie stepped under the boarded window, and Gwen followed. I squatted to the concrete to look through the opening. "Is this stable?" I crawled through the small opening.

"It doesn't need to be stable, just discreet," Gwen got my attention from the snack section.

I began to walk up and down the aisles, and everything seemed to be un-expired. I looked over at Gwen, and she just smiled. "This is all survivalist food that travelers come and get. Ellie replenishes the stock often." I felt more at ease; this seemed to be a very calm and quiet place.

"Say, Ellie, how do you make profit, if you don't mind me asking?" She smiled and walked towards me. Ellie snatched my arm and pulled me towards the public restrooms. It smelt horrific, but behind that door was something that was going to change my fate forever.

Chapter Eleven:

I held my breath and went through the old restroom door. It was just a dark black room. I looked over at Ellie and Gwen, who were both in the room with me. Ellie took a key from the inside of her shirt and locked the door, with multiple locks. "What's going on, Gwen?"

Gwen smiled wide, almost creepily. "You'll see…" All of a sudden, Ellie hit the light switch and the floor dropped from under us.

I began to scream my head off. I managed to glance over at Ellie and Gwen, who were in the military position, and they were just as silent as they could be. I kept screaming and screaming until we reached the bottom of the shaft. I thudded into the foam pit at the bottom, and Gwen and Ellie just laughed.

"Seriously?" I was baffled at how dangerous that was, and how Ellie could run a place so secretive like this.

We walked down a dark hallway and through some black curtains. Ellie and Gwen went first, and the crowd behind the curtain began to go wild. Then I heard Gwen over a loud speaker, "And now, my fellow revolutionaries, I present to you, the woman who single handedly took down the spy and is the key to ending this worldwide tyranny. I give you, Jayleen Tane!"

The curtains opened and a whole bar full of people was just watching me. They all just stood there in awe, and then they all screamed and cheered. I walked up to the mike, "Uh… hello." The crowd laughed in amusement. What was so funny about that? "I'm Jay Tane, as you know. I am the daughter of the late Rick Tane, and I plan to fulfill my father's dream of freedom for everyone on this earth."

The crowd roared and cheered. They began to chant, "Jay! Jay! Jay! Jay!"

I jumped off the stage and went over to the bar. The bartender looked at me. "So what'll it be?"

I laughed. "How about an ice water?"

He looked at me confusedly, "What's so funny?"

I smiled. "Oh, nothing. It's just I haven't been able to sit at a bar and drink a nice glass of water in a long time."

I began to think back upon the times I spent with my brother Garret. He was seven years older, so he was a major influence on me. My brother was the one who taught me how to fight and how to fend for myself in the wilderness. I remember one instance when he was teaching me how to shoot with a rifle, and the first shot caused me to fly backward. He just stood there. I began to cry because I was only ten years old at the time, and he was seventeen. "Look, Jay, sometimes we misinterpret certain situations that occur in life and have a low expectation. Now, in this instance, you thought that this would be easy, correct?" I nodded with dried tears still on my face. "Well, life is actually a lot harder than we think it is. You have to test it out, become experienced, before you can know things. Now try it again."

He held out his hand for me. I stood up and took the rifle from his hands. I aimed towards the target and pulled the trigger. I flew backwards again, but this time I didn't cry. I just got back up, and kept doing it over and over again until I didn't fall. My brother taught me so many things, and I just wish he was still here to help me. I know that he'd know what to do right now. For the first time in my life, I didn't have a single clue what to do.

A young man approached me with wide eyes. "So, Jayleen, I am curious on what your plan is to stop the XYZ Men in their tracks."

I chuckled. "Sir, you can call me Jay, and I am going to find my family first so that we may plan this together."

The man scuffed his shoe on the floor. "Excuse me? You're just going to go off and find your stupid family before saving the world? You're saving a handful of people before you save billions of them? I guess now we see where your priorities are, Miss Tane."

I stood up from my seat. "Now hold on, sir, I will not put up with that tone you're using with me. And, yes, my family comes first because we are the sole benefactors to the Rebellion. After all, my father did create it. So before you go around accusing me of doing something wrong, make sure what you're argument is solid."

His eyes began to widen even more by the second, "Ah, I see, Jay."

I laughed again, humored by his immediate humility, "Now you may only call me, Jayleen."

I sat back down on the barstool and put my head down. I was emotionally and physically drained.

"So what's up with you, kiddo?" Sam, the bartender, asked with such a sarcastic tone that I didn't even want to respond to him.

"Oh, nothing, just that about two thirds of the world is counting on me to save them, and I don't even have a plan. That's all."

He laughed. "The thing is, Jay, you don't really need a plan. All you need is for them to believe you have a plan, and just do whatever your heart tells you to do."

I brought my head up, "Ok, what I don't get is why a bartender sounds so smart?"

He laughed and turned around to fix someone a drink "Well before the XYZ Men shut down the colleges for the underprivileged, I was on my way to getting a masters in psychology. Since they only have college available for the wealthy children, I do not have a degree. But I know all the material."

This is what they've done to our world: they took the voice away from intelligent minds just because they're minorities. "The XYZ Men must be stopped, but I am just one person. How am I supposed to start this revolution?"

Sam leaned in and whispered, "Your father and mother have already started it; you just have to finish it."

I nodded. "Okay, well, how am I supposed to find my siblings?"

Sam leaned back behind the counter, "Oh, you mean David, Eddie, Luther and their two friends?"

I jumped out of my seat. "Yes! Do you know where they are?"

Sam pointed his dish rag across the bar to a booth where my brothers sat, looking fatigued.

I ran across the bar to my brothers. I jumped over a couple people to get to them, but once I had gotten there David acted as if he didn't see me, but I ignored him. "Luther!"

He turned to me and screamed, "Jay!" He ran into my arms and hugged me tight.

"I've missed you, little buddy, are you okay?"

He smiled through his tears. "I am great!"

I haven't seen Luther so happy since before mom and dad passed. I looked over at Eddie, and he was reading a book as usual. "Eddie!" I yelled. He looked up from his book and put on his glasses so that he could see me.

He jumped up and ran to me. "Jay!" He and Luther held onto me tightly.

"Why didn't you guys come let me know you were here?"

Luther spoke softly, "Because David told us not to."

I walked over to sat beside David and put my hand on his shoulder. "Good to see you, old friend."

David turned to me, "Oh. It's you."

I laughed. "Well, that wasn't the welcome I was expecting... Are you all right, David? Luther told me about how you made them stay here."

He spit into his cup and shook his head, "We all were doing just fine."

I nodded. "So nothing happened with those two while I was gone?"

He shook his head again. "Nope."

I shook my head back at him. "Well, something is about to."

I stood up and walked towards Matthew. "So Matthew, how are you?"

He stood up and hugged me. "Oh, Jay, I am so happy to see you! Are you all right? You look banged up."

I laughed for a second, and then I shoved him up against the wall. "So when were you going to tell us that your father is Dr. Z, you traitor?"

He rolled his eyes. "Jay, I wish you hadn't found out so soon. I was just getting to know your family, and now I bet you're going to either kill me or leave me out in the storm for dead." He paused. "Wait, where is Mark?"

I just kept staring at his eyes. They were filled with lies, and I could see it now. Before I couldn't because I was blinded by their fake kindness, but now I can see the evil and hatred.

"Jay, did you kill my brother?"

I kept staring, and I didn't say a word.

The teenage boy began to cry as I had him pinned up against the wall, "You killed him," he cried out.

I let the boy go, and he fell to the ground, "I never knew who my father was, but Mark did. My mother was very poor, and in order to find a good path to a good life and an education, she somehow married Dr. Z." He sniffled and wiped his face, "She never let me near him, but one night Mark snuck out and found him. My father planted seeds of world domination into my brother's mind. He became sick with the power of evil. He went on a rampage and told my father that my mother had cursed his name. Then she disappeared forever." He began to cry again but stopped himself. "One day, Mark decided that we would both go on an adventure for father, to find you and your family. It took us two years to find you all, and once we did Mark had a plan for our father to capture all of you. The mission failed, and we only received you. The council decided that you and Mark would compete in a death match. You won, so they set you free. Did a man ask you where the Rebellion Headquarters was?"

I nodded. "Yes, but I told him the wrong place."

He gasped. "Jay, they must know by now that you lied. They will be coming for us all!"

I just sat there, "Well, not you."

He looked up from the floor. "What?"

I looked down at him. "They won't be coming for you, right?"

He laughed, "Oh, yes, they will. Because I will tell you this:" Matthew stuck his finger in his ear, and I heard a click, "Jayleen Tane, the XYZ Men have planned to attack us in two night's time in this very town. Do whatever you want with this information." Matthew took the device out of his ear and put it close to his mouth. "Oh, and, Father, if you're listening, this is for my mother." Matthew took the earpiece out and slammed it onto the ground. He took his foot and smashed it to pieces. "There. Now we must find someplace safe to stay. Get going before they find us."

I slowly got up from my seat and helped Matthew stand. "We need to leave." I walked across the bar to Gwen. "Hey, something came up, and we have to leave now."

She looked so confused. "Wait, is your family here?"

I nodded. "Yes, but, Gwen, we really need to leave now. The XYZ Men plan to attack the town in two days, and we need to evacuate."

She ran towards Ellie and whispered in her ear for a good minute. Ellie nodded. She and Ellie shared a long hug, and Gwen jumped up onto the stage.

"Okay, everyone, listen up. Gather your belongings and go with Ellie to the shelter. You mustn't inform anyone that you are leaving. It is important for everyone's safety that we all follow my directions and nobody panic. Everyone's lives are on the line." Whisper's and the sound of shuffling feet filled the room. Gwen went over to Ellie once more to give her a hug. She left her there, on the other side of the bar, alone once more.

"I'm coming with you all," Sam said, jumping over the counter.

Gwen smiled. "Sam, I need you to help Ellie group everyone into the shelter, please do this for me."

He smiled. "Okay, fine, but if you run into me soon I will join you all." Sam turned to me, "And, Jay, remember what I told you tonight."

I grinned a little. "Okay."

We all went up the elevator/death trap, which was a lot less exciting than the way down. Luther began telling me how funny it was to see Eddie go down the shaft and how much he screamed. Once we got to the gas station floor, we grabbed some water canteens and packaged foods.

Sam came running after us. "Wait!" We all turned towards him. "Here," he tossed a set of keys to us, "use my car, I don't need it anymore." I jostled the keys in my hands and pushed the unlock button: a large, black vehicle's lights went off. I gathered all of my siblings and friends, and we went off into the night.

I jumped into the driver's seat, and Gwen hopped into the passenger's seat. All my brothers and the two newest members of our little broken family filled the large car. "Wow, this is a nice car." I was baffled that he had just simply given this to us.

Gwen laughed. "Well, he is a very nice guy, and I've known him for a fairly long time."

I nodded. "You two seem very close. Is there anything going on there?"

She giggled franticly, "Oh no! He's like a brother to me. Besides he's almost ten years older than I am!"

I laughed, "Wait, you're eighteen?"

She smiled, "Shh! I don't like people knowing I'm so young…"

I glanced over at her. "Gwen, nobody cares how old you are, you know, and age doesn't really matter anyhow."

She smiled. "I know, but we all have our snags."

I raised my eyebrow. "Snags?"

She grinned at my unknowingness. "Everyone has their snags, things that snag us and make us either uncomfortable or upset."

I nodded. "Gwen, you know this place better than I do. Where can we go to be safe for a couple days?" She sat there silently, like she didn't have a clue what to tell me. "Guinevere?"

She looked over at me. "Well, there is this one place… It's a day long drive, but it's secluded. There's just one problem…"

I laughed. "Oh, come on. It cannot be that bad."

She made a very alarming face. "Depends on what type of person you are, I guess." She laughed. "When my parents and I came to America, we bought a mansion in Texas to house our many relatives."

I slowed down to a stop at the crosswalk, "Uh… What does that have to do with anything?"

She smiled, "Oh, you'll see."

~ ~ ~ ~ ~ ~

We finally arrived at the mansion after an eighteen hour car ride, and I was exhausted. I got everyone out of the car and had to carry a sleeping Luther.

David complained, "This kid is heavy, Jay, why do you get the lighter one?" David shifted a sleeping Eddie on his back.

I put my finger over my mouth, "Sh. Wouldn't want to wake them up now would we?" Honestly, those kids wouldn't wake up if I wacked pots and pans together, I just wanted David to be quiet.

We stood at the front steps. Gwen rang the doorbell, and a loud gong sound crackled to life. "Oh, and don't let them see the fear in your eyes," Gwen advised, standing still in front of the door.

All of a sudden, it sounded like a stampede was coming towards us. My family stepped back from the door, although my brothers still didn't wake. The door creaked open. "State your business," a deep voice said.

"I am here for tea."

The door slammed, and from the other side all I heard was creaking and cracking, like locks unlocking. The door burst open and a whole ballroom full of people began to cheer: "Guinevere is home!" They pulled everyone inside. All of our mouths were agape. The walls were draped with grape-colored linens, and the walls themselves were made of the finest porcelain you had ever seen. There was a giant staircase to the right, and under it was a magnificent library full of the oldest books you had ever read. I just stood there in awe. I couldn't speak.

"Now if they ask you any questions answer them truthfully; most likely they already know the answer." Gwen put her hand on my shoulder. "You know, Jay, without you I wouldn't be here today. I am thankful I met you."

I smiled. "Oh, it was my pleasure to meet you."

"So, Guinevere, who are these ravishing…," the older woman looked at us up and down, "dirty people?"

Gwen looked at her with disgust. "These are my friends, the Tane family. And this here is Jay Tane, the girl who saved my life."

The family moved in on us like vultures and began asking my brother and I questions: "So, Jayleen and David Tane, what is your plan to get the world up and running again?" Gwen slapped her brother upside the head.

"Family, family. We have been in a cramped car for over thirty hours, so we must be left alone to sleep." I smirked at Gwen's lie to her large family. They all cleared the way for Gwen's mother, Mrs. Charles, to lead us up the stairs to our rooms.

"Now, I hope you don't mind our arrangements, but we paired Luther, Eddie, David, and the Matthew boy in the same room, and Guinevere, Jayleen, and the little girl in another room."

I nodded, "That sounds lovely, Mrs. Charles, thank you so much. Oh, and the little girl's name is Lu."

She smiled from ear to ear. "Oh, it is my pleasure dear, and nice to meet you Lu."

I walked down the hallway to the boys' room to put Luther into his bead and kiss him and Eddie goodnight. I stopped in the middle of the hallway because a familiar sight caught my eye. A painting that my father had in our cellar was on the wall. I stared. "Hey, is this original?"

He nodded. "Beautiful, isn't it? Like you."

I smiled. "Why thank you. What's your name again?"

"Benjamin Charles. Gwen's brother." He held out his hand for me to shake, "But my friends call me Ben."

"Well Benjamin, it is nice to meet you."

"The pleasure is all mine Jayleen," he smiled at me, which made my cheek's blush.

"You can call me Jay, Benjamin."

He laughed. "As long as you call me Benjamin, I shall call you Jayleen."

I nodded. "Duly noted Benjamin."

As I walked down the hallway towards the boy's bedroom, I began to think about that painting on the wall. My father would sit under that painting and tell us stories of how he would one day win the battle against the "bad guys" and save the world. Every time he would tell us the same story: "One day, I was just sitting there, and BAM the bad guys broke into our house. They tried to take you all away from me. But I said, 'No, this is my family! And if you want them, you have to go through me first!' And I used my fist and smashed all of their faces one by one, kids. Remember, if anyone ever tries to take something you love away from you, fight for it with all your heart."

I tucked the two boys into bed and said, "Goodnight, my little warriors." They both were still passed out, but it just felt right to tell them that. Before I left I went over to David. "Come with me for a second, please," I tugged on his shirt as a gesture to follow me. He got up off his bed and followed me to the enormous kitchen downstairs.

I got a cup and began to make coffee. "Would you like some?"

My brother shook his head. "I still don't like it."

I laughed quietly to myself. "Sorry, you know how weird I am." He smiled for once, and it was an honest smile, too.

"What normal person has to drink coffee in order to sleep?"

I laughed at my brother's witty comment. "Well, who said I'm normal?" He smiled again. Twice in a row I got David Tane to smile! I couldn't help but smile, too.

"You know, Jay," David paused, "I actually was terrified while you were gone."

I stopped sipping my coffee. "What?"

He looked at his feet. "I thought you were going to die. And I couldn't stand it. I cried for the first week you were gone. I couldn't stop thinking about you not being here, Jay. The boys need you. Hell, I need you here!" David began to tear up, but held them back. I put my cup down, walked over to my brother, and I hugged him. The last time I hugged my brother was when we were not ten yet, and it was family picture day. He was forced to hug me, though. This time, he actually hugged me back. My brother seemed different from his usual self; he seemed happy.

Chapter Twelve:

The next morning was calm. I found out the night before that my brother actually has feelings, and it put my mind at ease for me to know that he was all right.

I walked down the stairs in the clothes that Gwen's mother had laid out for me. Everyone was already at the table except my brothers. "Good morning, Jayleen, how did you sleep, dear?" Mr. Charles bellowed from inside the kitchen.

"I slept wonderfully, Mr. Charles, thank you for asking. How did you all sleep?"

The whole Charles family looked up from their five star breakfast and said in unison, "Well."

I smiled. "Wonderful." I sat down in the seat labeled with my name, "These are wonderful placemats. Pure silk?"

Mrs. Charles laughed. "Why, yes, my dear! Such a good eye! I wish Guinevere would catch such things and speak more like you, Jayleen." Mrs. Charles shot a look at her only daughter out of five children.

Gwen simply smiled at her mother. "Well mum, you should be happy with me being more diverse than the average woman, like Jayleen also."

I winked at Gwen, "Oh, yes, Mrs. Charles, your daughter is a wonderful girl and a very handy person to have when you're in the woods." Mrs. Charles wasn't buying anything I was selling. I filled my plate with eggs, ham, and some hash browns.

Mrs. Charles giggled. "Oh, Jayleen, it is already eight o'clock! Where are your darling brothers, my love?" I smiled at her, knowing that basically she just told me to go get them up because they're lazy.

I complied with Mrs. Charles. "Oh, yes, I will go get them, Mrs. Charles."

I quietly got up from the table and went up the stairs to the boy's room. I knocked on the door, but I didn't hear a sound. I opened the door to see all three of my brothers snuggled up together in a tiny bed. I smiled and proceeded to wake them up. First, I went to Luther and put my hand on his shoulder. "Hey, bud, you ready to wake up?" He turned over in disapproval. I went to the other side of the bed to wake up Eddie. "Eddie, time to wake up!" He did the same. Finally, I went over to the very edge of their dog pile to David. "Hey, David, wake up, dude, it's already past eight." I shook his arm. He didn't budge either, but he tried to hit me in the face.

I had to come up with a civilized way to wake my three brothers. I walked over to the bathroom next to the room and filled up a tiny cup of water. "This should do it," I walked back into the room of the three little bears. I stuck my fingers into the cup to get the tips of my fingers wet. I pinched my fingers together and then flicked the water at David's face. "Achoo!"

David pulled his hand out from under the covers and touched his face, then looked at his hand like he had to confirm that his face was wet. "Ew!" He jumped up from the bed. "Nasty children!" He ran to the bathroom to wash his face, and I just sat there laughing hysterically at my brother's reaction. I did the same trick to Eddie, but he wasn't as big a drama queen as David; he giggled at me and put on his clean clothes. I picked up Luther and let him sleep a little longer on my shoulder.

I walked down the stairs with my three brothers, but everyone had gone except Gwen and her brother, and they both were washing dishes rapidly. Gwen turned to us, "Oh, so sorry, Jay. They all had an important meeting to attend, but I can whip you up something!"

I put my hands up, "No, it is quite all right, Luther has an acquired taste anyway. Would it be all right if I cook them all something?"

She nodded, "Nothing is off limits here!"

I smiled, "Thank you, Gwen."

For the next thirty minutes, I fixed eggs, bacon, and some mashed potatoes for Luther. The child has an acquired taste, but, hey, the kid knows what he wants. I have to respect that.

After breakfast I made all the boys take showers and get cleaned up. I walked downstairs to ask Gwen a question, and I heard Mrs. Charles on the phone. "Now Harry, she's fairly ragged around the edges, but she is the most powerful young woman in the world right now!" She stopped talking for the first time since I've been here, and then began to describe me: "She has a dark pigment with yellow undertones, long, dark brown hair, and she has an unsightly tattoo on her shoulder of roses." She paused for a moment. "Oh, Harry that sounds wonderful! I will bring her right away." She hung up the phone and went into the kitchen. "Jayleen," Mrs. Charles shouted, "Come here, please, dear!"

I came around the corner. "Yes ma'am?"

She smiled and took both my hands. "Jayleen, we have a gala here every year, and this year's is tonight. We would love it if you would join us as the guest of honor!"

My eyes widened. "Oh… okay, Mrs. Charles."

She threw her hands into the air, releasing mine. "Oh, goodness, dear! If we don't hurry we'll be late for the spa appointment!"

I widened my eyes even larger. "*Spa appointment?*"

She laughed. "Oh, yes, my dear, Guinevere went through this process her first gala, and so shall you, my dear!"

I smiled and looked to the stairs, "But what about the boys?"

She smiled and looked above to the railing at the edge of the overhang on the top floor. "Guinevere will watch them, dear." Mrs. Charles pulled me out of the door and into her car.

"Since we are considered royalty, they think of us as XYZ Men followers. We just let them think that, but, dear, we must change your look to help get some of the tension off. I think it is time for a change."

I shrugged. "I guess that could help. Do you mind telling me what they are going to do?"

She grinned devilishly. "Oh, my dear, a miracle is what they're going to do."

Chapter Thirteen:

The car ride to the salon was fairly bumpy; we spent about an hour driving there. Once we were out in the middle of nowhere, Mrs. Charles pulled her car into the woods. I looked over at her in confusion, "Mrs. Charles? Why are we in the woods? I thought that we were going to some fancy spa for that gala thing." She stopped the car in front of this beautiful tree and got out of the car. I proceeded out of the car. "Mrs. Charles?"

She turned to me quickly. "Jayleen, this is top secret. If anyone hears you, we could all be executed."

I closed my mouth. "Yes, ma'am."

She walked up to the tree, she ran her fingers down the trunk, and she began to speak softly. "Do you see this tree, Jayleen?" She didn't even let me answer her question. "This is where the magic happens, Jayleen." Mrs. Charles took hold of the tree branch, and suddenly the ground moved out from under me.

I screamed. We fell down more than two stories into a dark hole in the ground. Finally, we fell into a foam pit. Mrs. Charles didn't say a single word, or make a single sound on the way down. I honestly was tired of being dropped down shafts for no reason.

We walked into the darkness from the pit and Mrs. Charles pressed a red button on the side of the tunnel. "Get ready, Jayleen." A gigantic metal bolted door swung open, and a bright white light shined on us. Mrs. Charles already was walking into it. "Aren't you coming dear?"

I smiled, "Yes," I stepped into the light. For some reason, since the first time I saw Mrs. Charles, I trusted her.

We walked into a giant salon. Everything was white and modern, and looked extremely expensive. Then suddenly, a fairly short, bald old man came scurrying towards us. Mrs. Charles greeted him, "Theodore!"

"Mrs. Charles! Such a pleasure to see your glowing face again. And you must be Jayleen Tane." He held out his wrinkled, tiny hand for me to shake.

I shook his hand. "Nice to meet you, sir," We walked past a makeup station, massage station, fashion station, and then Theodore led me over to the hair station.

"Now, Jayleen, I am going to go get a massage while Theodore buffs you out. If you have any problems or preferences, talk to him, but I promise you my dear, he's a professional."

I smiled. "Yes, ma'am."

I sat in uncomfortable silence as the stylist combed his boney fingers through my matted hair. "Jayleen, is it?"

I nodded in half approval. "Yes, but I'd prefer that you call me Jay."

He smiled like I had said a funny joke. "Here you are known as the person who could save the world, you know." He pulled his hands away from my hair as quickly as he could. "But this hair could take over the world. Have you even gotten it blown out before?"

I shrugged. "Uh, what's that?"

He buried his head in his hands. "Oh, my, I have my work cut out for me, don't I?"

I nodded. "You sure do." I smiled at his aged face through the giant mirror in front of us. "I believe in you, though, Mr. Theodore."

Theodore smiled at me. "All right, belle, let us begin."

Theodore had the most patience I had ever seen in one person. He took the time to brush out my hair and wrap this little foil-like strip into my hair with a paste in it. After he had covered my whole head in these foils, he stuck me under a large bowl that was super-hot. I had to sit there and wait, and wait, and wait until a loud alarm went off. Theodore came back to the bowl and took it off my head.

Theodore brought me back to the hair station, "Now since we are getting close to the end of your transformation, I need to blindfold you, just so that the reveal is more exciting!" Theodore seemed as if he hasn't been this excited in a long time.

"Do whatever you have to do, Mr. Theodore." I smiled at his excitement, and then he blindfolded me. He began to rinse my hair in a giant sink, and then he applied a fresh smelling soap. I hadn't had a nice bath with real soap in forever, not until Mrs. Charles took us in; my brothers and I hadn't had a home since our parents were around.

"Oh, Theodore, where's Jayleen? You were supposed to keep her until she was completely finished!"

Theodore chuckled, "Madam, I present to you, Jay Tane, the girl who will save the world and look gorgeous while doing it."

The curtains I was hiding behind were pulled open, and I saw myself for the first time since I gotten here. I knew then that I was not the same girl I used to be.

Chapter Fourteen:

We arrived back at the mansion and there was nothing there. I expected cars to be piled up in the front, yet it's empty. "Mrs. Charles, where is everyone? You told me there was a gala tonight," I asked her confusedly.

She laughed and whispered, "My dear, look closely." Mrs. Charles pointed at a patch of green out in front of us. The patch of green grass moved and twitched. "Jayleen, it is a cloaking device we use to hide our wonderful guests during our gatherings. If someone who was involved in The XYZ Men drove by and saw... Well we'd all be seven feet deep in the ground!" I shuttered as she slammed the car door.

"This long dress itches like crazy, when may I take it off?" I wined as we walked up the steps, although I mainly clutched to Mrs. Charles arm because of the high heels Theodore insisted upon me wearing tonight. They even put fake hairs on my eyelashes to make them 'pop.'

I'd never really been the type of girl to wear the pretty clothes, apply makeup, or even do my hair in the morning before school. My family never had much money, so getting hot pink dresses to fit in with the other girls at my school wasn't ever an option.

Wearing that gown made me feel like a princess. When the curtain opened and I saw myself, I hardly recognized who I was. Theodore had finally decided on dying my whole head this really bright blonde color because he said it was, "A commanding color, and it brings out your tan." I honestly would've been fine with him just leaving my rats nest alone, but I guess he was correct. It's a bold color, but still modest. He slicked back my hair while it was straight as pin needles.

I've only ever worn a dress three times in my life. The three times I've worn a dress were at my graduations. I barely count them as dresses. They were things donated to us – probably out of pity – but I believe that if it were about pity, they'd be nicer dresses. The dress Theodore picked out for me is very well fitted, but the bottom of the dress flairs out into the 'trail' of the dress, as I heard Theodore call it. The dress was strapless, and had jewels all over it. The royal blue silk rubbed my skin the wrong way, but I guess I could manage to wear it for one night.

The makeup look Theodore made a little woman do on me was called: "the fierce cat eye." I find the name quite funny, but when I laughed at it Theodore shot me a look; I guess that wasn't the intended reaction. They put all these creams on my face, including this one that was the same exact color as my skin. Then they smeared dark colored neutral powders on my eye lids with little puffy brushes. And then he pulled out a small pointed pen and tried to poke my eyes out! Then he attached small hairs to my eye lashes. *Who does that?*

I walked up to the front doors of the mansion with Mrs. Charles. I began to feel overwhelmed with emotion, like I was actually scared. "Mrs. Charles… I don't know if I can do this."

I looked over at her, and she took a deep breath. "Dear, here's a lesson I taught Guinevere a very long time ago: you must not let your fears take over your life. Sometimes you have to throw all of the fear you have out the window and forget about it for a minute and enjoy life! So let's get in there and give them the fearless Jay Tane!"

I smiled with a tear running down my cheek. "You called me Jay." I wiped the tear away.

Mrs. Charles took her hand off of the door knob and hugged me, "Dear, I realize you don't have a family anymore. But you do now. I already consider you a Charles."

I smiled. "Thank you, Mrs. Charles, but…"

I paused and didn't finish my sentence. "No buts, my dear." She pulled away from me gently and put her hand on the knob again. "Are you ready to give hope?"

I smiled wide through my fear and threw it out the window. "Yes."

Chapter Fifteen:

We walked through the door and over to the large staircase. We stood over the whole party, and everyone was conversing below us. The ballroom was filled with beautifully dressed women and finely dressed men. I spotted my brothers right away; they were all cleaned, sported fresh haircuts, and all of them were in fitted suits. I saw Lu and Matthew in the corner near my brothers; they were both dressed up, too. I looked around to see if I could find Gwen, but she wasn't with them.

I felt a cold and clammy hand on my exposed shoulder, "Jay... you look beautiful," Gwen's accent trailed off. She, too, was wearing a beautiful gown, but it was golden yellow. It brought out her ash blonde hair, and she seemed stunned by my appearance. "Let me guess. Theodore?"

I smiled. "He was lovely." She took my hand and started towards the stairs. I didn't walk with her; I just stood there in my uncomfortable heels.

"Well, aren't you coming? We have to show off that beautiful dress and hair somehow, Jay; don't let fear get the best of you. Throw it." I threw my arm back and motioned throwing an object and smiled.

As we made our way down those steps, every step I took down the iron staircase, a little bit of fear escaped my mind.

I remember when I was little, I used to fear everything. And when my mother and father died, along with my older brother, my fears were confirmed. Life isn't made for being scared; it is for living in the moment and doing right for the world while you're still here.

Everyone in that ballroom looked up at Gwen and me. They all gasped. I heard a couple of whispers: "Who is that girl with Guinevere?"

"I have never seen such a beautiful dress before, is that their cousin?"

"Wow, look at her!"

I have to admit, the compliments felt really flattering.

Mrs. Charles tapped the head of her microphone. "Hello? Oh!" she chuckles, "Hello, everyone, and welcome to the Rebellion Banquet!" She pauses while everyone applauses her soft spoken words. "Now, we have a very special surprise guest at our banquet this year. May I introduce Jayleen Rick Tane!" She set down the microphone and clapped. Everyone around me begins to applaud the announcement, too, and cheer also. They all gravitate towards Gwen and me, wanting to converse. Mrs. Charles took the microphone off the stand again. "Now, now, everyone give her some space! Jayleen will be making a speech at the end of the banquet, so let her enjoy the party! Everyone welcome her and her family with open arms!" The guests applaud once more, then the orchestra begins to play and everyone started to dance.

I made my way across the dance floor to my brothers. As usual, they're sitting, doing nothing, except Luther, who runs to hug me. "Well, hello there, little gentleman. To whom do I owe the pleasure?" I curtsied to my little brother.

He giggled and said, "My name is Luther Tane. Would you like to dance?"

I smiled. "Oh, I would love that, kind sir."

I took my brother's hand, and we made our way onto the dance floor. We danced for one song, and then Eddie joined us. We danced and danced and the boys told me jokes they had learned from Mr. Charles while I was away. We all laughed. It was like I was in a wonderful dream that I never wanted to end. Everything was so wonderful until Gwen's older brother, Ben, interrupted us: "Excuse me, but may I have a dance with the lady?"

My brothers scowled at him. "What's in it for you?"

Ben put his hands up in the air. "Nothing, just wanted to dance with someone who isn't my mother or sister, or someone who's over thirty."

My two brothers laughed and went around playing with the other children. I made my way to the dance floor with Ben, who honestly didn't strike me as 'attractive.' Sure he was handsome, but his personality seemed too distant for me to understand. "May I?" He was meaning to gesture to dance with me, but I had to think about what he was asking.

"Yes, but I must let you know I have two left feet." I smiled and looked down at my feet that were in the uncomfortable heels still.

He laughed, "Oh, it's quite all right, Jayleen, I can teach you how to dance. But only if you would like me to." He smiled. It's about the only thing I like about him at the moment: his smile.

"Oh. Okay." I said it hesitantly. But he looked happy anyway.

"Okay, so just follow my lead. Ready?" I nodded slowly, and we began to step back and forth, swaying in rhythm with the rest of the men and women at the banquet.

"So, Jay, when will you be leaving us?"

I slowed my steps. "Well, honestly, I don't want to ever leave. It's wonderful here, and the boys like it so much. I don't want to take it away from them. They need structure, you know?"

He nods in agreement. "I see, but what about – you know – saving the world?"

I smiled and began to stiffen up. I tried not to think about that, but I guess that I can't throw that thought out of my life like my fear. "Oh, yes. I will have to come up with a solid plan to take the XYZ Men down once and for all. It might take some time, though." My voice trailed off into my own thoughts.

He smiled and put his hand under my chin. "Jayleen, I didn't mean to upset you. Spend as much time as you would like here. To be honest, I have enjoyed having you here."

I smiled and shook my head. "Thank you," I laughed and continued dancing with Ben. He was a wonderful dancer and quite the conversationalist to my surprise.

We talked more about our lives and what our futures would've been if the revolution hadn't started. Ben said he would've been an architect and own his own company. I told him about my dream to become a lawyer and own my own law firm. He thought that I'd be great because I, and I quote, "Tell it like it is." I thought that was funny of him to say; he was actually a funny person.

Every once in a while Ben would gently intertwine his hands with mine, but I'd eventually pull away.

"Benjamin." I paused, "Would you help me with something?"

Ben stopped dancing. "Depends on what it is, Jayleen."

He walked with me to the snack and entrée table. "Well… would you mind helping me make a plan? I usually don't ask for help, but I'm afraid I have no choice in the matter now."

Ben put down his drink. "I'd be honored to work with you." He paused and tapped his fingers together. "There's one thing I want to promise you."

I stopped eating. "What is it Benjamin?"

"Someday, I am going to take you out on a real date."

I laughed at his gesture. "*Sure* you will. Should we go check on my brothers?"

Ben nodded with his disappointment. "Yes, I believe they are over there." Ben pointed to the statue of a giant tree across the dance floor.

My brothers were climbing on it like woodland animals, recklessly kicking at the tree and at each other, "Oh, no, Eddie! Luther!" I scurried across the dance floor. Ben followed.

Gwen pulled my arm, "Wait! I need to talk to you. *Now.*"

I smiled at Ben. "Would you please try to get them down for me?"

He smiled genuinely at me, "I'd be happy to." He walked across the dance floor and vanished into the sea of gowns and suits.

"So… I saw you and my brother hitting it off," Gwen elbowed me in my arm lightly. "You're very cute together."

I laughed aloud. "No, we were just talking."

Gwen smirked at my fib. "Jayleen. I see the way he looks at you. It's very flirtatious." She grinned. "And you can tell by his and your body language, so basically you gave it away."

I laughed. "No, Gwen. Besides, he and I were just speaking about him helping me create a plan to take down the XYZ Men."

She gasped. "I want to help!"

I smiled and put my hand on hers. "You were the first person I was going to ask, but before I had the chance he asked me to dance."

She giggled. "Then I guess the race begins! Who can keep Jayleen? Is it the dashing, smart, and beautiful Gwen, or her toad of a brother, Ben?"

We both laughed at her words. "Your brother isn't a toad; he's actually quite nice."

Gwen grinned at me again and just held the grin.

"Oh, okay, cut it out, Gwen!" We both laughed. I stood up from the bench. "Well, I must go find my brothers before one of them breaks something."

I walked across the ballroom towards my brothers. They both were still up on the tree, but now they were joined by Ben. "Boys!" I shouted.

A couple of women turned around to scowl at me for my bad manners. All three of the boys looked down at me. "Hey, Jay-Jay," Luther bellowed from the lower part of the tree.

He jumped, and I caught him in my arms. "What were you doing up there?" My tone was stern, but still soft. I didn't want to ruin that night, but they still had to be disciplined.

Luther smiled and looked up at me. "I love you, Jay-Jay, please don't ever leave me again."

I kissed my little brother's forehead. "I cannot promise that I won't have to leave again, but I can promise that I will come back."

Luther smiled and wrapped his arms around my neck, bringing me into a hug.

I put Luther down. "Eddie, it's your turn." Eddie looked down and stuck his tongue out at me. I laughed, "Do you really want to play that game with me, Eddie?" Eddie smirked devilishly, as if to say 'forget that, I'm going to ignore you.'

I looked at Ben, who had already climbed down, and he smiled. "It's all right. Besides, he's just a kid. They're bound to climb on things every once in a while." Ben put his hand on my shoulder. "Let's go make that speech, eh?"

I giggled like a tiny girl. "Okay." *Did I really make that sound?*

I walked alongside Ben as we climbed the staircase to where Mr. and Mrs. Charles sat silently. As we ascended my fear returned. *What was I going to say to these people? How am I possibly going to change the world?* I began to panic and feel lightheaded. I stopped at the top of the stairs, but Ben caught me. "Jayleen, are you all right?"

I attempted to smile, but my fear turned it into a frown. "I'm just fine."

He frowned back, "I realize you're scared and have the weight of the world on your shoulders, but my family and I are here to help you. *Watch!*"

Ben let go of my hand and walked quickly to the microphone. "Hello, everyone, my name is Ben Charles, as you should know. Let's get to the chase here, this banquet is about being a united front against the enemy, the XYZ Men." The crowd booed at the mention of the XYZ Men. "Now I know you are all wondering how we are going to eliminate the enemy, once and for all? Well, with the help of Jayleen Tane, we can make this world a free place again. The only way we can accomplish this goal is to use force; peacemaking isn't an option anymore. We must attack this head on. Here to help me explain it to you is our honored guest, Jayleen Tane." Ben took my hand and dragged me over to the microphone; I was shaking in my heels.

Ever since the third grade I had been deathly afraid of publically speaking. Even after the pep-talk my father gave me in the car on the way to school, I still felt uneasy. I went as far as to sticking the thermometer to a lightbulb to make it hot and acting sick. I got the, "Oh, sweetheart, we cannot

keep you out of school a whole day. We can just pick you up after your speech."
I groaned and stomped my sixty pound self to my room. My speech was over the
rainforest habitat, and I had rehearsed for a whole month beforehand. I walked
up to the booth my mean teacher had set up at the front of the class. My palms
were sweaty, my armpits were drowning in perspiration, and my head felt as if it
was a balloon full of air. By the time my speech was supposed to start, that
balloon popped and spewed air all over the front row of children in my class.
Ever since then, I had tried to avoid public speaking at all costs.

"Uh…" I looked over at Ben. He was right next to me, still holding my
hand. "Hello, everyone," I paused to take a deep breath, "I know you all are
worried about the future, but we cannot worry any longer. We cannot worry; we
must do something about it. That is why I am planning a war against the XYZ
Men to stop their reign of terror. We need as much help as we can get, trained or
not. All we need is people with passion and drive. I cannot do this alone. We
must do this together. Thank you."

I stepped away from the mik and looked at Ben. All he could do was
smile. "I am proud of you. I didn't even help! That was all you."

I smiled. "I wouldn't have even been able to get up the stairs without
you!" He smiled so wide that his cheeks looked like they were going to fall right
off his face.

My brothers and I danced the night away. I actually enjoyed myself,
though I still had the thought of going to war in my head throughout the whole
night; it haunted me. I couldn't stand the thought of my family being in danger
again. After what had happened with Mark, I didn't trust anyone anymore.

The banquet ended around midnight. I was very tired and had had one
too many pieces of chocolate cake. I must admit, I have a weakness for
chocolate.

Ever since I was little, I would walk my brothers to the grocery store.
The store had three large candy machines at the front, and all it cost to have a
sweet butterscotch candy between your teeth was a dollar. I gave each brother a
dollar, and Eddie would always ask, after our walk to the store, "Can we
surprise daddy with his favorite when he gets home from work, Jay?"

I would smile at him and say, "Okay, fine." We'd walk over to the pastry section, and I'd make each brother ask for the "German chocolate cake special." We'd get the cake and walk the three miles back to the house, set up the cake on one of mom's finest china platters, and then wait for his arrival home from work.

And every time he got home he would yell, "Well, you kids spoil me, you know!" And then we would all tackle him with hugs and love. I miss my father more than anything, and I know he misses us, too.

"Jay, can we talk?" David knocked on the French door frame looking out over the outdoor balcony.

"Sure." I gestured him to join me as I watched the cloaking shield buffer as people moved throughout it.

David walked up to me in his nice, unwrinkled suit. He put his hand on my shoulder. "Jayleen," he paused. I was shocked that he used my real name. He knows I don't appreciate it. "I am worried about you." he held his breath as he spoke to me. "You're not yourself."

I raised my brow in confusion. "And what brought you to that conclusion?"

David sat down in the lawn chair next to me. "You're showing so much weakness, and you've been crying a lot. I can hear you at night. You sob yourself to sleep. Imagine if the enemy knew that! We'd be dead!"

I scolded him, "I have always done that, David. You've just been too full of yourself to notice. And it doesn't happen every night. It was just the night before last." I rolled my eyes in disgust. "You know, when we had that heart to heart, I thought you had actually changed. Ha! My mistake for having faith in you."

I turned to walk back inside when David grabbed my arm. "Now just hold on a minute, you little twit, don't go around throwing my name in the dirt. I honestly just want the best for you, Jayleen. You don't need to be crying and showing weakness because that will get you killed."

I laughed through my anger. "You know what David? I'm not going to let your negative attitude ruin this perfect night for me, therefore I am removing myself from this conversation."

I jerked my arm out of his grasp and walked away. I went down the stairs and vented about my talk with David to Gwen, and what she said to me has stuck with me my whole life. Gwen said, "Love this life that you have been given because it is the only one you have, even when it gets bloody, cherish it."

Chapter Sixteen:

I woke up the next morning in my bedroom. I hadn't cried myself to sleep the night before. For once, I went to bed happy.

"Jay!" Lu tugged onto my sweater. I was surprised; I had never heard her say anything. "Jay-Jay, it's snowing!"

I smiled and stretched, "Oh, really, well let me see!" I got out of bed, put on my sweatshirt and walked out onto my balcony. Everything was white. The crystal-like sparkles sprinkled throughout the blanket of snow amazed me. The snow was magical, and it was Lu's first. I went back inside and walked down the staircase. I saw from halfway down that Mrs. Charles was in the kitchen cooking breakfast.

"Why, good morning, Mrs. Charles! It smells wonderful in here." I smiled at her and sat down at the bar.

Mrs. Charles gave me a weird smile. "So do you have any interest in my son?" She held her frying pan in a tight grip.

I tensed up quickly. "Uh…" Her sudden question took me by surprise.

She smiled. "Dearie, I am not going to say anything to Benjamin," she put her hand on top of mine, "but I am just curious."

I rose my brow, "Uh, I'm gonna go see what my brothers are doing." I got up from the bar and walked back up the stairs. That was really awkward. *Why did she even ask? And why did she have to know about it?*

I got to the boys room and knocked on the door, "Hello?"

I heard footsteps and then my youngest brother, Luther, answered the door. "Hi?"

I smiled. "Did you notice what's happening outside?"

He looked at me with confusion. "No."

I bent down to his level. "*It's beginning to look a lot like Christmas…,*" I sang.

His eyes lit up like a Christmas tree. "Eddie! Come quick! It's snowing!" Both boys bounded down the stairs in long strides and burst through the front door to play in the snow with Lu and Gwen. I proceeded into the bedroom where my brother, David, lay, facing away from me.

"Dave?" He didn't even flinch. I walked over to his bed and put my hand on his arm. "David, I realize things got heated between us yesterday, but I want to talk about it with you."

David stretched his arms and turned to me. "Jayleen, I hope you realize that it is," he turned over to glance at the alarm clock, "noon and my brain isn't awake yet, so come talk to me after lunch. Then you'll get the answer you want."

I took my hand off his arm. "How about you get up off your ass like a normal person? Nobody sleeps in until noon anymore."

He laughed at me. "Ha, if you hadn't woken me up with your talking, I probably would've slept until five."

I rolled my eyes. "You're such a bum." I smiled after the fact. "Dude, seriously, why'd you go off on me last night?" I gave him my best concerned look.

He sat up in his bed and rubbed his eyes. "You haven't been yourself ever since you had to kill Mark. I am worried about you getting feelings so quickly. And you seem to have lost your edge." David got up and stretched his legs.

"Ew, put some pants on, weirdo," I threw his jeans at him.

He laughed at me. "But, seriously, I was just worried about you is all."

I smiled at my brother's compassion; he just doesn't know how to convey it correctly. I hugged my brother. "I love you. Don't you ever forget that." I felt his cheek muscles tighten- maybe a smile?

"I love you, too, sis." He squeezed me tightly.

"And if you need any help with anything, let me know," David said genuinely.

I smirked, "Well… I think you just gave me an idea." David and I stared at each other, and I could see that he knew what I was talking about.

Chapter Seventeen:

Every adult and teenager gathered around the table in the kitchen. The children were upstairs watching a movie.

"Everyone, I have called you here today to discuss a plan." I tried to speak with grace so that no one would be scared. "I have devised a plan to take back the world from the XYZ Men, but it isn't going to be easy."

Every person around the table nodded. David pulled out a map and sprawled it across the wooden table. "We shall form an army of rebellion members and sneak attack the main headquarters of the XYZ Men. Since Jayleen has been there, and we have Matthew who… knows about the territory…we drew a map to show where we will be attacking and taking over. We have taken the liberty of assigning leaders to each group already. Here are the groups:

Group A: Jayleen

Group B: David

Group C: Benjamin & Alfie

Group D: Gwen

Group Ambush: everyone else

"Group A will be in charge of taking over the main surveillance area, and this is where we will dis arm the whole building. Jayleen will be part of this team, and so will Matthew."

Matthew smiled. "I will do whatever you guys need me to do."

I explained Group B: "Group B will be taking over the guards around the perimeter of the building, and this will be led by David." I paused to let the groups sink in to their heads, "Now Group C will be one of the most important. Group C and group A will be taking Mr. X, Mr. Y, and Dr. Z into custody." I paused again, "And if they refuse, you have permission to kill." I took a deep breath and allowed everyone to nod. "I put two people I can rely on the most in charge of this group, Alfie and Ben," Ben and Alfie both nodded, but didn't say a word. "Group D will be releasing anyone who is in the LIU or the prison. I have put Gwen in this position, along with Mr. and Mrs. Charles." I sighed, "And, finally, the last group is pretty self-explanatory: Group Ambush is the leftover people who will ambush any guards on the inside because, believe me, they are everywhere. Okay, so any questions?"

Ben raised his hand. "So, what do we do with the three men after we capture them? Kill them?"

I shook my head, "No, we mustn't kill them unless they refuse arrest. They will simply rot in jail for the rest of their lives, stripped of their power."

Everyone clapped and left the table except Mr. Charles. "Sir, I couldn't help but notice that you don't look very pleased with the plan. Is there something you would like me to change?"

He shook his head. "No, sweet pea." He shook his head again. "It's just that I hope this won't be the death of me."

My smile faded. "Oh, don't say that, sir." I put my hand on his shoulder. "You still have plenty of time!"

He laughed. "No, dear, I don't. And secretly, between you and me, I'm ready to go." He pointed to the ceiling.

I smiled. "Sir, you don't mean that!"

He chuckled again. "I've been on this earth for sixty seven years. I'm tired. I've lived. Besides, and don't tell Guinevere this, I have the cancer."

I gasped. "Sir, you have to tell her!"

He shushed me, "No, ma'am, that little girl has seen things that no child should see during this war, and I won't add knowing her father is slowly dying to the list."

I hugged him tightly. "I'm so sorry, sir."

He smiled and pulled away. "Promise me one thing, Jayleen."

I smiled through my newfound sorrow. "Anything, sir."

"Make sure that when I die, I die for the worlds freedom."

I nodded. "You have my word, sir."

Chapter Eighteen:

I decided later that we needed to find a place to hold a meeting with Rebellion members to recruit people. So Ben, Gwen, Matthew and I got into the car and off we drove.

Soon after the awkward silence took over the car, I found myself lost in thought. I looked over at Gwen, "Do you and your family go to church?"

Gwen smiled. "Not since my grandmother died. Why?"

I put both hands on the steering wheel to have more control. "Well, I was thinking… it would be good for all of us to go to at least one service, just to see how it goes."

I secretly wanted her to say yes because church was one of the few things that calmed me. While my brothers and I where on the run, even without my parents, I would bring them to any church that we could find along the way. If it was being used and a service was happening at the time, I would set up a table outside the window so that my brothers and I could sit as a family at what we called "our own early service." And if the church was abandoned, we just invited ourselves inside and had our own service.

"Gwen?" I didn't want to back down on this. "Please!"

Gwen laughed a little bit which made her words sound muffled, "Okay, okay, we can go this Sunday."

I smiled and hit my hand on the steering wheel. "Yay! Thank you!" I smiled as wide as possible.

I looked into the rear view mirror to see Ben staring at me. Even when I saw him looking at me, he still kept staring. Gwen fell asleep about an hour ago, and has been snoring the entire time. One time she even said under her breath, as she was in the middle of a snore, "Is there a moose in here?"

I looked back at Matthew, and he looked very lonesome. "Matthew?"

He looked up at me. "Yeah?"

"Are you doing all right?"

He scuffed his lip on his hand. "Ha, yeah, I'm doing great for someone whose brother was killed last month, and by you I might add."

I sat up straight, surprised by his angry sarcasm. "Excuse me? Look, I am sorry. What was I supposed to do? Let him kill me?"

Gwen woke, her face pale over our topic.

"You didn't have to kill an innocent man!"

I slammed on the brakes in the middle of the road. "Innocent? I'd hardly call your brother innocent."

Gwen put her hand onto the safety handle. "Jay, please do not start."

I turned around to Matthew. "I am so sorry that your brother wasn't a good person, but that's not," I paused, "my," I paused again, "fault."

He crossed his arms in disapproval.

Gwen hit her fist onto the dash board and turned around quickly. "Look, you two ninnies. Stop fighting! I am sick and tired of hearing it, and everyone else around us is, too. Matthew, I am sorry your brother died, but Jayleen didn't have a choice!"

Matthew turned away and shut out everyone around him. And just like that, I was dealing with yet another teenage boy who hated my guts.

Chapter Nineteen:

I never had envisioned that I wouldn't have parents anymore, nor had I thought about having to raise my three brothers. Yet, here I am.

We drove down the road for another couple miles. "Uh-oh. I need to stop for gas." I turned to Ben. "You have the money, right?"

He nodded. "I'll do it. You guys stay in the car." We pulled off into an old gas station. I put the car into park and removed the keys from the ignition.

The car was spilling over with silence, and it began to gnaw at me.

"Hey!" Ben yelled from outside of the car. I looked in the rearview mirror, and there were two large men in suits confronting Ben.

I turned to Gwen and Matthew. "Get ready. They don't look like the kind of people we want to see right now." I turned away, took a deep breath, and got out of the car.

"Hello! How are you two fine gentlemen doing today?" I smiled at the men who remained straight-faced and dead-eyed.

Ben looked to me with wide eyes. "These two gents are fugitive hunters." He tilted his head towards their large guns in their leather holsters.

"Oh, well, why would these gentlemen want to talk to us? We aren't criminals," I laughed with sarcasm.

Ben looked at me, scared, then back at the men.

One man opened his mouth to speak. "We have been sent to capture Jayleen Tane and her family for lying to law enforcement. Have you seen her, young man?"

The larger of the two behemoths held up an old photo of me. "Young man, what's your name?"

Ben cleared his throat for a moment. "Benjamin Charles."

The man who was holding the picture spoke softly for his large size. "You'll get a sizeable reward, young sir, if you tell us where they are."

Ben smiled. "I don't know who that is."

My heart was pounding out of my chest.

The man stepped towards me. "Ma'am, have you seen this girl?"

I put my hand on my hip. "No, I haven't. Sorry, kind sir," I smiled at both of them.

The two men shook their heads. "It's a shame, too; we were going to get some extra points with the boss on this one." They looked at each other, then to us.

The other man spoke. "We was gon' get us a nice raise. He must really want this one, bad."

I laughed. "Well, what would your boss want to do with an itty bitty thing like her?"

The two men chuckled. But only for a second. "We don't know, ma'am, but he wants her."

Ben and I laughed nervously. "Well, we will call you if we run into her. Can we have a phone number?"

The men put their hands in their pockets and jostled about their contents to find a pen and paper. "Uh, y'all gotta pen?"

Ben motioned for one of them to accompany him to the back of the car. "Yeah, follow me." Ben led him to the back of the car to get the phone number that we would burn once we got back home.

After Ben jotted down the phone number, we hopped back into the car and drove home.

Gwen shot me a look of desperation. "Who were they?"

I sighed heavily. "They were bounty hunters, looking for me."

She gasped. "Oh. No, are you going to be ok? Do we need to move? We can move." She glanced at Matthew. "Did you send them here, huh?" She frowned at him. "If you did, I will do the same thing that happened to your brother to you, but it will be ten times worse. I've been to the LIU, and I am not afraid to go back." She turned back around and faced forward in her seat, tensed and angry.

"Gwen, please calm down. He had nothing to do with it. Even the ninnies out there told us that their boss told them to come find Jayleen. But they were too stupid and didn't notice it was her because of her drastic makeover!" Ben spoke softly from the back seat, putting his hand onto her shoulder to try and comfort his agitated sister.

"Pft! *No*, I shall not calm down! I will not!"

Ben retreated back to his seat. "Sorry."

I gave Gwen my signature look. "Please don't Guinevere." Her eyes widened when I used her full name. "None of this is anyone's fault, except the enemy's, so we cannot and *will not* let something as senseless as this set us off!

Come on people! This is what has stopped us all these years from ending this war once and for all!"

And, just like that, my body lashed forward, and my head violently hit the steering wheel. I tried to cry out in pain, but it all happened so rapidly that I couldn't say a word.

I blacked out. I only saw shapes moving around me. I smelled the thick black smoke that surrounded me. Nothing seemed to be in the correct place. Everything was thrown off balance, myself included. I began to feel severely dizzy. It was then I realized our car had flipped over, and I was upside down.

I blacked out for briefly. Then I could open one eye, and I could see Gwen, squirming helplessly, trying to free herself; her lack of strength prohibited her from doing so.

Again I blacked out, but later I heard voices, very thickly accented voices. I thought that they were angels taking me away. I could feel the cold air rushing through the broken windshield and hitting me in my face, feeling as though it was sharp glass.

The only thing that I could make out of their words was, "Paul, we cannot just leave them here!"

I was afraid of both outcomes, *what if I die? Who's going to carry out the mission? And what if I live? Who's going to address my wounds?*

Then I saw my mother. She was at my window, and she began to break it. She used her fists, pounding on the window until it shattered. The glass hit my arm as I shielded my face. Surprisingly, I couldn't feel a thing, even though I knew it was penetrating my skin. My mother pulled me out of the car and placed me in the patch of snow on the side of the road.

I always knew my mom would be an angel, but I didn't know she was going to save my life.

Chapter Twenty:

I awoke violently, thrashing in a strange bed. I took inventory of the room it was dimly lit and filled with deer carcasses. I had an IV inserted in my arm.

There were bright pink curtains on either side of me. I began to squirm, and an older woman approached me from across the room. "Sweetheart, please don't move; you were heavily injured during the crash." Her thick southern accent was apparent.

I sat up in my cot. "I am not in the hospital, am I?"

The middle-aged woman in a silk blouse smiled at me. "No, honey, if we had let you stay out on that road much longer, the guardsmen would've surrounded you like vultures!" She giggled quietly to herself. She returned to her normal smile. "My name is Ruth, ah Ruth Burrows," she put her hand onto my shoulder to attempt to comfort me.

I turned to the curtain beside me. "Where are all my friends?"

Her face went expressionless. "Well..."

I frowned. *"Where are they?"*

She shook her head. "Dear, I didn't want to be the one to tell you this but..." Her voice trailed off, and then a large man walked into the room.

"They're all dead," he said with a thick southern accent that I could barely understand.

I went into robot mode: no emotion, no expression, and no reaction to the news that I had just received.

~~~~~~

I jerked my head up, and the room was darkened. I was in the same room, but it was nighttime. I realized that it was all just a dream.

I sighed with relief and realized I could see Ben from across the room. "Buh-Buh-Nun." I slurred. I jumped, *why can't I speak?* Ben lifted his head to look at me and then fell back into bed.

I looked at my arms. They were heavily scratched, and one arm had been stitched closed. My leg was bandaged tightly, as was my foot. I swung this foot over its partner and plopped the bandaged one onto the floor. I put my weak arms behind me and pushed off the cot. I put one foot out, and then the other, and then *splat*. I fell onto the floor. "Agh!"

Suddenly, under the door, I saw a yellow light flicker on. Shadows of feet appeared in front of the door, and I heard the thumping of them hitting the wood floors.

Then, the woman from my dream opened the door and flew to my aid. "Honey, are you all right?" I looked up at the woman, who was wearing a silk night gown. She picked me up and put me back into my bed. For such a little lady, she was pretty strong.

Once she had put me back into my bed, I finally got a word out of my mouth: "Friends."

She smiled at me. "They're recovering also. No need to worry, you will get to see them tomorrow at breakfast time. For now, honey, you need to rest." She pulled the blue sheets over my arms and placed a heating blanket over my midsection.

I slowly drifted off to sleep, my trust withering away into nothingness. I trusted no one, and nothing, even if the person saved me from the side of the road; people always have other intentions.

Chapter Twenty-One:

The next day, Mrs. Ruth, the middle-aged woman who had been caring for me, came up to the room and wheeled me out. The room was empty, but it was filled with five cots; only four looked used.

She wheeled me down the hallway and into a dining room. It was really big, considering how small the cabin was. I was sat at the end of the table, and Gwen was at the other. The two boys, Matthew and Ben, were on either side of the table, staring into nothingness.

Gwen's eye was bandaged and her arm was in a sling.

Ben seemed to have nothing wrong with him until he stretched his arms. His abdomen was heavily wrapped. He gasped for air and grabbed his midsection.

Finally, I looked over at Matthew, whose head was wrapped up in such a way that his head looked like soft serve ice cream. He also had this weird breathing machine hooked up to his nose.

Gwen and Matthew didn't have wheelchairs, but they were just as beat up as I was.

Mrs. Ruth scurried into the dining room with a tray of eggs, bacon, tortillas filled with toppings and a pitcher of orange juice. She laid the tray in the middle of the table. "Now, everyone, don't shove it down y'all's pie holes too quick cause ain't no way you'll return from that." She smiled at each of us, and then left the room.

Gwen was the first of us to speak. "What in the bloody hell happened to us?!"

Matthew pointed at me. "It-it-it's h-he-her-r f-f-fault," he stuttered severely.

I shook my head. "No." That's probably the only word I could say clearly.

Ben shifted in his wheel chair frantically. "It's no one's fault; we just need to figure out where we are."

Gwen crossed her one arm over her sling. "I honesty do not care where we are, just how we are going to get ourselves home!" Gwen threw her free arm onto the table. "And who are these crazy people?! Get me bloody out of here!" Gwen screamed and hit her hand onto the table again.

"Child, you better calm down before we tether you down to that gosh darn chair." The man from my dream walked into the room with his breakfast, and glared at Gwen for creating a scene.

Gwen took her fist off the table and opened her mouth to shove some eggs into it.

Mrs. Ruth walked into the room with a pitcher of milk. "Hello, everyone! How y'all doin'?" She smiled at the man. "I see y'all have met my Paul."

"Who are you?!" Gwen screamed at Mrs. Ruth, and she was quite startled by it.

"Honey, please do not yell. This house is small enough for us to hear every breath you take, so we can definitely hear you when you scream." Mrs. Ruth put the pitcher down. "My name is Ruth, and this is my husband, Paul, and we saved your lives! You know, when we first saw y'all on the side of the road, Pauly told me not to stop the truck, but I said, 'No, we have to pick those children up!'"

Paul interrupted her babbling. "Quit chit-chattin' with these here children, they need'a talk amongst themselves, and thank the lord above that they're livin' and a breathin' right now." He gestured for his wife to follow him to their living room, and she just smiled and followed.

Mrs. Ruth popped her head into the room. "I'm sorry about Pauly. He's just not used to visitors, and if y'all sweethearts need anythin' just say somethin'!" She went away and didn't come back for a while.

We all four sat in silence and ate all the nice food that Mrs. Ruth made for us.

Ben backed out from under the table, and wheeled himself towards me. "Jayleen, how are you?"

I felt around my arm, then my stomach, and then my head. "I seem fine! How is your stomach?"

He shook his head. "When we crashed, the tool box under the front seat flew open and one of the screw drivers hurtled toward me and…" He pointed to his abdomen. "But hey, now I have another great story to tell!"

I laughed at his optimism. "Yes, but we do need to figure out what exactly happened."

He nodded. "Mrs. Ruth seems to have taken a liking to you, so you should talk to her." He pointed down the hall. "Her study is right down that hall. Make sure to knock on the door frame. She likes it when people show good manners."

I smiled. "Thank you… for everything. For not letting those bounty hunters get me and, you know…"

He smiled wide, put his hand over mine and gripped it tightly.

I notice that one of his teeth was chipped from the crash. I tried not to stare, but it was just right there in my face; I couldn't help it. "Uh… did I do that?" I pointed at his chipped tooth.

He felt around his mouth with his tongue and made a surprised face. "Oh! It's no big deal, an easy fix!"

I smiled. "It was my fault." My smiled deteriorated. "I'm so sorry."

He shook his head at me. "No, no, no. It wasn't anyone's fault. In fact, it was ice on the road that made us lose control."

I shrugged. "I was driving, and I should've kept everyone safe." I wheeled myself out from under the table down the designated hallway.

Once I got to the end of the hall, I knocked on the door frame. Mrs. Ruth looked up through her ruby-red reading glasses. "Yes, darlin'?"

I twiddled my thumbs in nervousness. "Mrs. Ruth, may I please speak with you?"

She smiled and took off her glasses. "Oh. Of course." She threw her hands at me in gestures while she was talking; *I guess she talks with her hands.*

I wheeled into the room and situated my wheelchair. "We never really formally introduced ourselves. My name is Jayleen Tane."

Her eyes opened wide as saucers. "The Jayleen Tane?" she whispered under her breath. "Oh my goodness almighty, we have a celebrity in our house! My goodness gracious, how'd you get all the way down here, sweetheart?"

I smiled. "My friends and I were looking for a place to… set up shop." I decided not to tell Mrs. Ruth of our plan because let's face it, I barely know this lady, and I don't know her real intentions.

She nodded her head in agreement. "Yes, and I believe you had a question for me?"

I nodded my head. "Yes, ma'am. What exactly happened when you found us? Did you see us crash?"

Mrs. Ruth sighed. "Well, Pauly and I were driving down the road tryin' to get home after a nice trip into town, and we saw a car go swerving by, it flew over the side of the road after nearly hitting us! We slammed on the brakes, got out of the car, and saw that your car had flipped over on the road. I told Pauly we just had to help you. When we saw that you were children, I told him we just couldn't let these gifts from the Lord above die a cruel death. So, since Pauly and I both were E.R. doctors in our prime years, I told him we could nurse y'all back to health. He told me that we should just call the authorities, but I said, 'No Pauly! They could be taken to the L.I.U. so we needa heal them, otherwise they'd die one way or another."

She paused and took a sip of her freshly made coffee.

"Now I am one for havin' structure, and I just don't think that our government is good for anybody! I-I mean, these people have no idea how it is being regular people! They're just up there drinkin' their nice liquor and toasting to stupid things like bein' rich. Money isn't everythin' you know sweetheart, it's the people who you're with, not the objects you have. You can replace things, but you can't replace people. Well I guess you could. I mean when I was a little girl I dreamed of makin' me a cloning machine and cloning my favorite boy at the time. His name was Benjamin Mick, and I just thought he was the most gorgeous thing I had ever seen! But then I met Pauly and it was love at first sight. Well no… Actually I couldn't stand him when we were kids: he would always pull my hair and call me names. I guess that's just a way for boys to flirt with ya. But then, after a while, I got used to him and we've been married for thirty years! I'm only forty eight, but, hey, I look good for my age!"

Mrs. Ruth went on and on, talking about the most random things. Just when I thought I could squeeze in a word, she'd already moved on to the next topic.

"Oh!" Mrs. Ruth practically yelled from across her desk. "I've been talkin' your ear off! I'm so sorry, honey bunch. Would you like to tell me a little about yourself?"

I shrugged. "I don't know if you'd wanna hear that, Mrs. Ruth."

She laughed aloud. "Oh, honey! I live for tellin' stories! Lemme hear it!"

I honestly didn't want to talk about myself, because then I'd probably get asked a personal question about my parent's or about how my brother died; I didn't want to deal with it.

"Well… I guess I should start from the beginning. I raised my three brothers starting at the age of seventeen, and I have been the only thing there for them since. I was going to college, but that was cut short when this whole constantly being on the run began. I honestly don't know why, but I feel as if God has purposefully taken away my parents and brother to make me realize how strong I really am."

I took a long pause, shaky breath.

"Ha, when I was younger my father told me that my strength is stronger than anyone else's power." I wiped away a small tear that had trickled down my cheek. "He also told me to never give up, because there's always a light in the darkness; you just have to look."

She put out her lip in sympathy. "Oh, honey, I didn't mean to upset you." She put her hand onto mine again. "I'm here whenever you need me sweetheart."

I wheeled out and went back upstairs to lie down. I got myself up into my bed, and I could finally do it by myself.

Just as I had gotten into bed, Ben came next to me, finally able to walk normally. "Hey, Jayleen, how are you doing?" He smiled and stroked my messy blonde hair out of my face.

I smiled at his soft hands gliding across my skin. "I'm doing better. What are you doing?"

He grinned widely. "Well, Jayleen, I am going to take you on that date I promised."

I raised my brow. "I'm sorry, *what?*"

He smiled, took my hand, then helped me out of bed. "Just come with me." He slipped his hand behind my back and around my waist, and I put my arm over his shoulder. We walked down the hall to the back door. As we were nearing the door, Mrs. Ruth stopped us.

"Oh, no, where do you think you're going, missy? Benjamin, remember what we talked about?" Mrs. Ruth was beaming with excitement.

Ben nodded. "Yes, of course." He handed me over to her. "You have an hour, Mrs. Ruth!"

She nodded vigorously, "Yes."

We walked down the stairs to the large master bedroom. Mrs. Ruth's bedroom was spacious, and neat. She brought me quickly to her bathroom and sat me down in front of the vanity. "I'm going to fix you up for your date with that fine young man out there!"

I smiled. "Oh, Mrs. Ruth, you don't have to do that."

She put her hands on my cheeks and squeezed them. "Yes, I do!" With that, she began to throw things around in a whirlwind, with makeup, hair products, and clothes going everywhere.

Finally, after what seemed like forever, she finished.

My hair was curly, which is new for me. I had dark stuff around my eyes, which Mrs. Ruth called a 'smokey eye.' I just agreed with her since I know nothing about makeup.

After all that, she pulled out a red, tight-fitting dress from her closet. "I wore this on my very first date with Pauly." Her voice trailed off. "And since I don't have a daughter to give it to, I want to give it to you."

I smiled and held the dress in my bruised hands. "Thank you, Mrs. Ruth. I love it."

She smiled. "Good, dear. Now, go get your man! My time is up."

I walked with Mrs. Ruth back upstairs and to the back door. I went out into the covered outdoor porch, and Ben was sitting there waiting for me. Once his eyes met mine, he grinned as wide as he could. "Wow…" he paused. "Jayleen, you look amazing."

I smiled. "Thank you, Benjamin." I sat down across from him, settling in the padded chair, wearing my dress I had just received.

"Jayleen, do you know why I had this planned for you tonight?"

I shook my head. "No."

He smiled and took my hand into his. "Because ever since you first walked into my parent's home, I knew that I needed to have you in my life."

My cheeks turned bright red. "Oh, that's so sweet." I squeezed his large hand, which completely covered mine.

"This is the only food I could find around here…" Ben turned behind him and pulled out a platter with the usual hospital selection. "Mrs. Ruth wouldn't let me near her beloved oven or stove either. Ha."

I smiled genuinely. "It's perfect."

We sat there in blissful silence. My body was aching, my mind was tired. For that moment, though, I was at peace.

He talked about how he came to live in that mansion, and how scared he was when Gwen never came back. Then he brought up Mark.

"So what ever happened between you and Matthew's brother?"

I stopped eating and wiped my mouth. "He tricked me. He was working for his father, and he led me to be captured by the guardsmen. Then we were put in the arena…" My voice had become shaky, and I stopped talking.

Ben grabbed my hand and squeezed it tight in his. "You don't have to talk about it, Jayleen."

I bit my lip and proceeded: "No, I haven't talked about it yet, and I need to."

I took a sip of water and began.

"In the arena, the crowd yelled and kept chanting for Mark to slaughter me. I nearly died. I would have if it weren't for my dad. I swear I could hear his voice in my head, almost as if he was there with me. I suddenly became overwhelmed with strength and finished Mark. I wish I hadn't killed him."

Ben shook his head at me. "No. He was trying to kill you, so you had no choice, Jayleen. It's not your fault."

I clenched my hands. "I can't help but think that I could've helped him. I didn't have to kill him."

Ben looked agitated and angry. "Jayleen, don't ever say that. You can't help someone who doesn't want to be helped."

I frowned and looked down at my feet.

He reached over and slowly ran his fingers through my curly hair. "Don't be upset. This was supposed to help you, not make you sad."

"It has been wonderful, thank you."

Ben's smile made me feel warm inside. I looked closely and could see where Mr. Paul had replaced the front tooth that had gotten knocked out. He then caught me staring at his smile, so I awkwardly looked away from him.

He chuckled and still ate his food.

After I had finished, I put my napkin in my lap. Suddenly, Ben pulled out a small black rectangular object and clicked a button. Sweet classical music turned on, and Ben began to sway in his chair.

I giggled at him.

He got up from his chair and pushed it in. Then, he pulled out my chair and assisted me out of it. My body crackled as I got up, but I didn't care.

He slid his arm around my waist and helped me move awkwardly across the patio. Ben smiled at me, struggling. "Here." He lifted me up just enough to be on top of his feet.

"No. I don't want to ruin your shoes."

"Your pain is above any shoes."

I smiled and looked down at the floor. He laughed and squeezed my hand. I looked up into his eyes and just stared into them. We danced and danced, and then my favorite song popped on: "Hold My Hand (Duet with Akon)" by Michael Jackson.

That was my granny and my song. We would sing it together at the top of our lungs and laugh. It was her favorite song as a girl, then my mom's, and, finally, mine.

I smiled through my sadness from thinking about my grandmother and danced to my favorite song. Ben didn't seem to notice me zoning off; he just seemed to enjoy spending time with me.

"You know the night we had the gala? I was so nervous to talk to you." Ben woke me from my distant thoughts.

I raised my brow in surprise. "*Really*? You? Nervous?"

He nodded. "Yes."

I put my head on his shoulder as we continued dancing. "You have nothing to be nervous about. Trust me."

He leaned down and kissed my forehead.

I smiled and turned to see Mrs. Ruth standing in the doorway, staring. I looked at her with a grin on my face. "*Mrs. Ruth!* Have you been watching us the whole time?"

She giggled quietly with her hand over her mouth. "Just for thirty minutes or so."

I took my feet off of Bens' and sat down. "I need to go to bed." I yawned. "Thank you, Benjamin, tonight was just what I needed."

Ben walked to me, took my hand and kissed it. "It was my pleasure, Jayleen."

Mrs. Ruth walked me inside and sat me down at the kitchen table next to the backdoor. "Hold on, dear, I have to ask Ben something." She walked outside and closed the door shut behind her.

I slowly got up and put my ear up to the screen door. *What can I say?* I wanted to know what they were saying and if it was about me.

I heard Ben speak first. "Mrs. Ruth, I couldn't thank you enough. Tonight was magical. I wanted to make her happy, and I think I may have."

Then she spoke. "It was nothing, sweetheart! I love a good young romance! Now I had better get that girl to sleep. You don't stay up too late, you hear?"

Ben spoke again. "Yes. Goodnight."

Mrs. Ruth burst through the door to my surprise and caught me listening. She just smiled and took me to bed.

Once I had gotten into bed, my whole body released all its tension; I fell into a deep sleep.

~~~~~~

I woke up to the ringing of a large bell. I looked across the room to see Matthew had rung an emergency bell to summon Mrs. Ruth.

Mrs. Ruth came rushing to our room, shuffling her feet that were tangled up in some type of sandal.

Matthew started to get up from his bed and then had Mrs. Ruth guide him to mine. "Jay, may we please talk?"

I nodded and sat up. I patted my bed, and he slowly sat down at the end of it.

Mrs. Charles shook her head. "If we had, you know they would have found out what we were doing for the Tane's."

Gwen clenched her teeth and threw the glass against the wall; she began to sob.

I slowly hobbled to be by my broken friend's side. "Gwen, no." I tried to take her hand. But she jerked away from my grasp. It hurt to stand, I sat back down in the chair next to me.

"There wasn't any stopping this from happening, dear. Your grandmother had cancer, too. I just got it earlier than she did. There's no stopping *any* of this."

Gwen shook her hand up in the air. "*Why?*" she exclaimed, "Why *now?* Why *us?*"

"Stop it right now." I pushed with all of my strength, and I got myself up out of the chair. "Help me for a second."

Gwen stopped crying and gave me a look of disapproval. She then helped me stand up, and I slowly walked over to the couch with Gwen as my crutch. "We have lost sight of what is really important here: freedom. It doesn't matter if we're crippled or dying slowly. We *are* the only chance that this world has to not be suffering anymore. And if you don't see that, then you aren't in the right state of mind."

Matthew came to help me from the other side. "Jay is right. We need to stop feeling sorry for ourselves and complaining. We need to actually do something about it."

I nodded. "We have to stick together and take this head on, for Mr. Charles."

Everyone slowly nodded in unison. "For Mr. Charles."

Part Two

It's been a month since Mrs. Charles passed, and Gwen is still a wreck. Trying to comfort her didn't help much; she would just push me away and say that she's "fine."

Ben and I were with her when she died. We told her about our date we had and how wonderful Mrs. Ruth was. She beamed at the thought of Ben and me together.

Ben stood up to get water for her, and Mrs. Charles grabbed my hand and whispered. "Jayleen. Take care of my babies. Guinevere and Benjamin both need you. I can tell that you love them both so much."

I paused for a second. Love? *Do I love Ben?* I just put my hand onto hers and told her more about our date.

Ben returned with the water. She took a sip, and as we shared our experience together, she simply fell asleep. We thought she was napping, but then she stopped breathing. Ben began to sob. I called Gwen to her bedroom. Gwen came running and cried out to her mother's body, grasping her hands.

I put a hand on Gwen's shoulder. She fell to her knees and began to pray. Ben and I knelt to join her.

The next day we had the funeral. Gwen decided to have her mother buried next to Mr. Charles, under the same tree.

The ceremony was beautiful. Everyone, including my family, said kind things about Mrs. Charles. Everyone laughed whenever Luther described how his favorite memory of her was when she would make him "dinosaur cookies."

After everything, we arrived back at the mansion, now alone. It was midnight.

I tucked all the boys into bed and went down to the kitchen for my coffee. To my surprise, Ben was already there.

"How are you doing?" I gave him a slight smile.

"Better than I thought I would be."

I sat across from him at the table. He looked down into his cup of alcohol and laughed. "I have a question."

I put my cup of coffee down. "Yes, Benjamin?"

"Why?"

"I'm not sure what you're asking."

"Just why?"

"Benjamin?"

He put his head down into his arms. He mumbled something, but I didn't hear it. He then lifted his head and rubbed his eyes. "I don't get why all of this is happening. First, my freedom, then my parents, and now you'll have to leave soon. It's getting hard to stay optimistic."

I slid my hand across the table and intertwined my fingers with his. "Everything happens for a reason, Benjamin. And I'm not going anywhere, at least not alone. You're coming with me. I need you in order to succeed."

He sighed and sipped his drink. "All I know is if you hadn't come into my life, I wouldn't be here today."

I smiled and looked at his tired face. "You need to get some sleep. Off to bed!"

He chuckled at me. "Okay, fine. Goodnight, Jayleen." He walked over and kissed my cheek.

I smiled as he walked toward the dark hallway. I too, went to my bedroom to sleep. This time, though, I didn't really sleep. I just had darkness in my head. No dreams, no anything just nothingness.

~~~~~~

We had been to ten places already, and had recruited nearly three thousand people to join the rebellion. I stopped using people to assist me in walking about two months ago, and even when Mrs. Charles was at her worst, she helped me get stronger each day. She would even take me and Ben out for a stroll before dinner each night to gain strength.

Once I had been able to heal my wounds of grief from Mrs. Charles passing, I felt as if it was time to begin planning for the take over as we had before. I made some alterations to the list of people, of course, but the plan remained the same.

"Once we get out to the main facility, what should we do, Jay?" Ben seemed confused about the entire plan.

"You should get your squad together and wait for my signal."

Ben nodded slowly as if he were soaking up the information I had just given him.

Sunday came, so I forced the boys out of bed and into their Sunday clothes. I limped towards the front door to let the boys outside to the van.

When I felt a cool breeze from the outside glide in between my fingers, I closed my eyes and took it all in. Even though I'd experienced hardships and lost many people along the way, I was blessed to wake up to see the sun rise and fall another day. *What more could I ask for?*

We piled into the van and sat in sweet silence on the way to the church building. It was only David, Eddie, Luther and me because Ben and Gwen prefer not to go to church.

Once we had arrived, I stepped out of the van slowly. As soon as I began to walk, the crisp forest air gracefully entered my nostrils and exited through my mouth.

I sighed in relief and walked confidently into the abandoned chapel. The three boys followed closely behind me. As I walked into the building, a feeling rushed up and down my spine, as if someone had poured cold water down my back. I turned around, but nothing was there.

I hurried to the front and sat down at the end of the first row of seats. I bowed my head and took Luther's hand into mine. He squeezed my hand tight in his clammy hands. I opened one eye slightly to look at him, and he was clenching his eyes shut as tightly as he possibly could.

I began to pray aloud to each of my brothers, allowing them to take in what I was saying. "Dear heavenly Father, thank You for this blessed day on earth. You continue to bless us in many different ways by allowing us to walk, talk, hear, see, and more. We walk these grounds in Your faith, and seek peace on this earth. Please watch over all of us who are about to go to battle, for we need You now more than ever Lord. Luther what do we say next?"

Luther loosened his grip for a moment. "In Jesus' name we pray, amen."

Our heads lifted and our eyes met. "I hope you know that I love you all so very much." I came close to my three brothers and hugged them tight.

I knew that there was a chance I may not ever see Eddie or Luther ever again, and that was the scariest thing of all.

A legacy that my father left had to be fulfilled and I had every intention of doing so. Many innocent people had died because of being "different" in economical ranking or purely because they don't look appealing to The XYZ Men. If we didn't change that, then who will?

I had exactly a week to train over five thousand people to fight against The XYZ Men's army.

Once my thoughts subsided, we loaded up into the car and drove back home. On the way there, there was still a spell of silence, but this time it was a positive silence. It wasn't forced, nor was it due to fear; it was pure positivity.

We arrived home, and after tucking Luther in for his Sunday afternoon nap, I actually decided to take one myself.

My dream was very morbid. All I could see was death, blood, and loss. My mind was racing with possible outcomes that could occur, and it made me sick. It was all becoming so real to me: if I screwed up, the whole world was as good as gone.

My palms began to sweat, and I tossed and turned in my bed. I started to sweat all over, and a cold hand calmed my nervousness.

I woke up quickly to Eddie, who was looking down at me with sympathetic eyes. "Oh, I'm sorry, Eddie, I didn't mean to…" Eddie interrupted me and hugged me tight. I smiled and hugged him back. "No matter what happens, I'll always be here for you, bud."

Eddie crawled in next to me and fell asleep. So did I. We both slept peacefully, even though we both knew what was going to happen soon.

Chapter Twenty-Three:

I took a deep breath of the cool air. I loaded everyone into the van, and we drove back to Club Nine.

As we all rode down the icy road, the air in the car became crisp with anxiety and sadness. I knew that I would have to leave my brothers behind, and I knew that I may not ever see them again. After losing my parents, I didn't want to lose more people whom I love.

We were greeted by Sam and Ellie, our old friends, when we arrived at Club Nine.

We unloaded the car and hugged our friends. Then we traveled through the upper level of Club Nine and grabbed food for our trip. Eddie and Luther plopped their five-pound bag of candy and other sweets onto the counter. "Ring us up Ellie!" Eddie stood there excitedly.

"You're joking, right?" I laughed at my brothers. Just looking at their faces made me want to cry.

We returned outside. Sam and Ben went into the trees and whipped off a large green and black tarp, revealing a massive cargo plane. On the tip of the pane it read: "XYZ 309."

I stood in awe of the colossal plane as Sam just marveled at his prized possession. "This is my *favorite* trophy I've taken from those…" he paused for a moment, "…things."

I gazed at the plane, too. *How could he have stolen a cargo plane?*

We boarded the plane, and the boys ran ahead to take a tour of the cockpit and cabin.

They scampered about the plane, smiles broad and eyes wide. I marveled at my beloved brothers and thought about how much mom and dad would've loved to be there. How they would've loved to watch them grow up, to watch them have children, to watch them do all the things that they'll miss.

Everyone said their goodbyes. The boys gripped onto me tightly when I said they had to stay with Ellie.

Eddie didn't cry at first, but Luther bawled until we took off. I didn't want to let them go, but I knew I had to; it wouldn't have been fair to them. Before I left I took them both in my arms and whispered, "Now remember, Ellie is going to be me for a while. If you need anything, just ask her. I love you both so much. And..." I began to cry as well. "I may not come back."

Ben approached me from the plane. "Jayleen, we need to go."

"One second please." I smiled through my tears. "But, remember, we're doing this for freedom from the bad men. You be good for Ellie, you hear?"

"Yes." They both said while crying.

I took them into one last embrace, and stood to my feet.

The airplane rose, and I watched each forest pass quickly, looking the same as the last: icy.

It all became clear and real. If we didn't succeed, we'd be done for and not only let our parent's down, but the whole *world* down. All the people we'd met along the way, all the people who believed in us across the world would be doomed to a life of nothingness.

As all of this hit me like a train, I began to panic. I got up from my seat and ran into the bathroom and sat there. I looked up to the ceiling of the bathroom as I shook with fear. "Mom?" I began to whisper. "Mom, if you're listening, please watch over me today. I need you now more than ever, a-and I can-can't do it with- without you!" I sat on the disgusting toilet and was still.

"Jayleen?" Someone knocked on the door. "Jayleen, let me in please."

I wiped my eyes and opened the door slightly to see that it was Ben. I opened the door more. "Sorry, do you need to use the restroom?"

He tilted his head toward me. "No, I don't need to use the loo. I need to talk to *you*."

I sighed and opened the door all the way. "Come on in, Benjamin."

He smiled. "I think you're the only person besides my parents that I allow to call me that."

I smiled through my tears. "What did you want to talk to me about?"

He sat down on the bathroom counter. "I just wanted to let you know that you aren't alone in this."

He smiled and continued. "You have thousands of people who are cheering for you, and maybe even some that work for the enemy. You can't focus on all the bad in this, your parents wouldn't have wanted that for you, and neither would mine."

I started to cry again, but this time Ben came and held me. I slowed my breathing and looked up at him. "How much longer until we're there?" I asked.

He shook his head at me vigorously. "That doesn't matter right now."

I stared up into his wide and kind eyes, and our heads began to come closer and closer, until I pulled away.

He smiled. "Come with me."

I wiped my eyes with my sweatshirt's sleeves and got up off the toilet. I followed Ben down the stairs to undercarriage of the plane, and he brought me to the very tip of the plane where we were below the cockpit.

"What is this place?" I walked into a giant library with books plastered to the walls. He smiled childishly. "This is my secret sanctuary. Sam showed it to me, and I wanted to leave you here to rest until we arrive."

I walked along the shelves, allowing the books to lightly glide across my fingertips. "These books are fascinating!" I beamed at his kind gesture. "I'll stay in here. Thank you, I appreciate you."

He grinned and started to walk away, but then he paused. "Oh, and Jayleen?"

"Yes, Benjamin?"

He smirked at me. "If we don't die today, you and I are going on a proper date."

I walked over to him and hugged him for a long time. I needed it. "You can count on it." I gave Ben a kiss on the cheek, then returned to the couch.

Chapter Twenty-Four:

I heard heavy steps on the stairs. "Jayleen," Ben paused momentarily, "It's time."

I smiled at his faith-filled face. "Let's save the world." I replied sarcastically.

We landed in what my grandma told me was Hawaii when she was a little girl, but by then it was known as the forbidden fortress. It was a beautiful place, but it'd been under The XYZ Men's power for too long. Their presence had taken its toll on the beloved place.

We marched to one of the nearby caves where all the members of the rebellion had gathered before the battle. As the thousands of people rushed in, it all became surreal.

I took a deep breath and walked up to the podium set up for me. "Everyone, everyone, settle down. Many of you know me as Jayleen Tane, daughter of Rick Tane, and only some of you know me as Jay, the loving older sister just trying to raise her brothers right."

I took David's hand in mine and squeezed.

"But, today, you will know me and everyone else in this very cave to be the people who saved the world!"

There was no clapping because we didn't want to be discovered, but by all of the nodding heads and tears of pride rolling down their cheeks, I could feel the power of faith in that cave. People of all races, generations, different religions, and ways of life in one area standing up for what's right: it was a magnificent thing, I'll tell you that.

We separated into sections and initiated our march towards the headquarters. Heavily armed from the remains of the cargo plane, we were ready to fight for freedom. The grey skies parted, and the sun bled through the white fluffy clouds and peered down on us.

I felt the presence of my parents, and Mr. and Mrs. Charles marching along with me and my team. We marched quietly up to the tall stone building in our all black, sleek uniforms.

I signaled everyone to get close to the wall, and I counted down with my fingers: five, four, three, two, one.

I raised my gun in the air and fired a shot of war. "Long live the Rebellion!"

As we charged up the walls, the only sound you heard for miles was thundering and the beating of hearts hungry for freedom. Gunfire rang throughout the island, and so did cries of mothers, fathers, brothers, sisters, sons, and daughters dying. I have never heard anything more horrific than that sound of war. My group scaled the wall. After my last man was over, we charged up to the very top floor, killing whoever got in our way, and made our way to the master's suite.

A man ran out and jumped onto me. I turned, and stabbed him in the chest. He fell over, but not without cutting my leg with a knife. My adrenaline blocked the pain from processing with me. We continued on.

By the fourth floor, I had lost twenty men out of one hundred. And by the eighth floor, I had lost forty, but the enemy had lost more than I did.

By the final floor, I had just thirty men left. We crept towards the giant doors and burst through them to attack.

The room filled with smoke and gunfire, and as the three leaders fled the room, I signaled ten of my men to follow. We hurried across the room to the door from which they escaped, but we cornered them; they were trapped. We killed the three guardsmen and tied Mr. X, Mr. Y, and Dr. Z together in three chairs. The three men glared at me with disgust in their glazed eyes.

Chapter Twenty-Five:

"Hello, Jayleen, nice to see your darling face again. Too bad you changed some of your appearance so we couldn't have met again sooner," Mr. Y said, flashing a truly evil grin. "These are my associates, Mr. X and, your favorite, Dr. Z."

I shook my head with a chuckle. "Oh, sir, why the comfortable tone? Are you not tied up and held at gun point? Are you not under attack by people who have nothing to lose, yet everything to gain? Sir, your positivity is inspiring and all, but I'm afraid that you're not going to get anywhere with it." I walked towards him, and slid the side of my dagger across his neck. He shook with fear.

Dr. Z sat up in his chair and straightened his legs. He had a long beard and white hair that cascaded back into a slick pony tail. "My dear, we have a million guardsmen on site and then some. Are you so sure that you, a little orphan girl, are going to beat us?"

I chuckled at his remark. "A little orphan girl." I turned to Matthew, who was standing quietly behind me with his mask on. "Dr. Z is it?" I slowly walked towards him.

The man nodded confidently. "Indeed."

I smiled and crouched down so that I was eye level with him. "You have two young boys, yes?"

He nodded. "Mark and Matthew."

I nodded slowly. "Yes, and where are they now?"

Dr. Z stopped talking and his head fell. I took my dagger and put it under his chin. "You know where they are. You're just in denial. The only son that loved you is dead because of me. The other is standing behind me, waiting to hear your last breath, because you made him feel like he wanted to be a," I paused, "little," I paused, "orphan," I paused once more, "boy." I took my dagger out from under his chin, and his head fell completely, and he began sob.

I turned to the last of them. "And I don't think I've made your acquaintance yet. Jayleen Rick Tane."

I held my hand out for him to shake, but he spit into my hand and then onto my shoe.

I laughed. "Oh, my, you'd think that a so called 'leader' would have more class than that." I sheathed my dagger and took out my gun. "My grandmother used to tell me that sometimes in order to defeat evil, you must become evil. But, to never lose sight of my mission, do you, sir, know what my mission is?" I kneeled down to become face to face with Mr. X.

His eyes met mine and he said slowly, "No."

I smiled and said, "Long live the rebellion." Gunfire rang, throats were slit, and blood spilled. All three men died in those three chairs. After the leaders were successfully executed, we ran out of there and headed back to the ground floor.

As we ran, I looked outside the window to see a field of blood and not many survivors. I took out my radio. "Sam, are you ready with the plane?"

I waited for his reply, and the radio crackled to life. "Yes, Ben and Gwen are accounted for. All we need are you, David, and Matthew." I began to panic as I ran; I knew where Matthew was, but not my brother.

We got down to the garden and to the plane. One by one, my last five men went up the rope, and I brought up the rear. Then I saw a familiar face on the ground below me.

I froze in the air. *"David!"* I looked up at Sam, who was staring down at me, and then I waved to him. I dropped to the ground and rushed to my brother's aid. "What happened?" I cried out to him.

He shifted to look at me. "One of the guardsmen stabbed me in the shoulder and in my leg." He choked on his words. "Go without me, Jay. I'm dead weight."

I shook my head as tears rolled down my cheeks. "No, David. You're my family; I can't lose you. Eddie and Luther need you. *I need you.*"

He smiled and put his hand on my face. "Jay, I don't know why you were my sister, because I didn't deserve to have you. Make sure you tell Luther and Eddie that I love..." His head dropped, and his chest stopped moving. His hand then fell from my face and thumped on the ground.

I cried out and rested my head on his lifeless chest. Then I felt a cold hand on my shoulder. "Jay, we need to leave now."

I turned to see Sam behind me, but this time he looked familiar to me. He had sweat splashed all over him, and his hair was turning jet black, like he had spray-painted it. "Garret?"

I stood up from the ground. "Oh, Garret!" I ran to him and held him. "I thought I'd never see you again."

He pulled me to his chest and hugged me. "I'll talk to you about everything later, let's get David onto the plane."

I wiped my tears and helped Garret load David's body onto the plane. Blood was spilling out of his wounds and all over me.

As we climbed up to the opening of the plane, I heard a loud pop. I kept climbing the ladder, and as I reached the top, a wave of relief graced me. I stepped towards my long lost brother to hold him, but my leg crumbled underneath me. I looked at the leg to see blood cascading down my black uniform.

The loud pop I had heard was a gunshot from the ground, and due to my adrenaline rush, I didn't feel a thing. But now I felt it. I grasped my leg and looked at David, then Garret. I off took my jacket and ripped the sleeve from it, tying it tightly around my leg to keep the blood from running.

"Jayleen!" Ben ran to me and sat on his knees. "You need to help her!"

I looked up at Garret. "Help David first."

He nodded and ordered some of his crew to take him to the couch.

Garret took a bag off the wall and dug through it. He pulled out a clear glass bottle, a few rags, and a needle and thread. He bit the cork of the bottle out with his teeth and spit it across the room. He then set it down and performed CPR on my lifeless brother.

I just sat there worrying. I had won the first battle, but I didn't know if I'd win this one.

Chapter Twenty-Six:

David shook as Garret pushed on his chest. "Come on kids!" Garret exclaimed. Then, as Garret put his lips on David's and blew air into his mouth, something happened.

David's eyes slowly opened. He smacked Garret across the face. "Dude! Quit kissing me, I'd rather die than have you kiss me!"

Garret chuckled. "Take this," he said as he stuck a wad of cloth in David's mouth. "You'll need it."

David raised his dirt crusted brow. "What?"

Garret proceeded by pouring the clear substance onto David's leg and shoulder.

David began to squirm and scream in pain. "What the hell, man?"

He kept screaming, and Garret stopped working. "David, keep that cloth in your mouth and bite down. I'm about to stitch you up, and I suggest you not look."

David's eyes widened, and he shook his head. "Just throw me off the plane! No way am I letting you stick a needle in me!"

Garret sighed and slapped David across the face. "Shut it, you're being stupid."

David clenched the cloth tightly in between his teeth as Garret weaved the needle and thread through the wounds and sewed together his gashes. He whined the whole time, and Garret laughed.

I was after David. Garret took some type of plyers and slid them into my leg. I cried out. "Can't you do it gently?"

He glared at me. "Do you want the bullet out or not, Jayleen?"

I rolled my eyes and sat back, trying not to look. As he stuck pliers in my leg, my eyes widened, and I grabbed onto Ben's arm next to me.

Ben whimpered. "It's okay, Jayleen. Take this."

He handed me a cloth to put in my mouth to bite on.

"Agh!"

I watched each forest pass by under the plane. The ice was melting off the trees, and the sun made another beautiful appearance in the sky above.

On the plane ride to Club Nine, everyone was celebrating our victory, tossing champagne aimlessly everywhere while laughing and cheering. I didn't join in the party; I just sat by the cockpit and waited to reunite with my other brothers.

"Jayleen, why are you sitting alone?" Benjamin emerged from the cockpit and sat next to me. "Aren't you happy? Your brother is alive! We won the war! We're free!"

I smiled. "I'm thrilled, but I cannot be happy until I see Eddie and Luther."

He nodded in agreement. "Yes, I see." He put his hand onto my shoulder. "I came to tell you that Garret wants to speak with you in the sanctuary." He took his hand away and smiled genuinely at me. He offered his hand to help me stand.

I entered the library and sat next to David on the couch. Across from us sat Garret, our missing brother. I took a good look at him. He had grown a small beard and had let his hair grow out since the last time I saw him.

"I have called you both in here to talk about my disappearance long ago. Are both of you ready to listen and save the questions until after I finish speaking?"

I always hated that about Garret; he had to act professional. I rolled my eyes. "Yes."

David looked at me, then Garret, and said "Yes," too.

Garret took a deep breath. "Dad and I were in the watch division, and they ambushed us after we had just arrived. Dad and I managed to get away from the attack along with another man, but one guardsman followed us and shot Dad as we tried to escape. I killed the guardsmen after I heard him shoot, but I couldn't save Dad in time. His wounds were too advanced for my abilities."

I spoke up: "But that doesn't explain why you were at Club Nine and never even told me that it was you!" I was getting aggravated with my brother, and by the look he gave me, he was aggravated with me, too.

"You didn't let me finish, Jayleen," Garret replied through clenched teeth.

I shook my head quickly. "Continue."

He cracked his knuckles. "I met Ellie while walking through the woods, and she offered me a job at Club Nine, along with a fake ID, a place to stay, and food. I didn't want to reveal myself to either one of you because I didn't want you to be distracted from your mission."

I nodded. "Well," I paused to try and think of something else to ask him. "Well," I stopped to think of something to ask again, but my brain found nothing. I got up from my seat and walked slowly across the room to hug my brother. I hadn't held him in years, but he still felt the same to me.

Chapter Twenty-Seven:

The plane began to descend, and my excitement grew. I couldn't wait to finally see my beloved family and reunite us all once again.

The plane tilted downward, and I couldn't hold it in any longer. I leaped out of my seat as soon as I felt the plane's wheels touch the ground and gathered my luggage.

The plane door slowly opened, and I jumped out, running to Club Nine. I burst through the door, and there sat my two brothers, playing a board game together peacefully.

I ran to them. They both looked up at me and screamed, "Jay! Jay!"

Tears began to roll down my face, but for once these tears weren't sad; they were happy. I was overjoyed, exhilarated, and happy to see my family together once again.

David and Garret both walked in and joined in the hug, too. My family was reunited, and everything in my world was complete.

Ellie walked up to Gwen and motioned towards me. Gwen jumped. "Oh, yes! Jay, you must broadcast our victory! The camera is right here. Just stand right there." She took me by the shoulders and guided me towards the spot. "And say whatever you feel is right."

I didn't even care to look at my appearance. Ellie stood behind the camera, counting down on her fingers: five, four, three, two, and one. She nodded her head telling me to begin.

I spoke softly. "Hello, everyone. I am pleased to inform you that our fight for freedom is over. We have a long road ahead of us, but we can get through it together. The hardest part of our journey is over. We will make this world whole again. We, as brothers and sisters, sons and daughters, friends and family, can do anything we put our minds…" I paused and thought, "and hearts to. I am proud of each and every one of you, of your bravery and courage." I stuck my swollen fist into the air and shouted, "Long live the Rebellion!"

I limped away from the camera as everyone in the room shouted in unison with pride: "Long live the Rebellion!"

After I had given my speech, my gaze turned to Benjamin, ear bandaged and face swollen.

I ran to him. "Ben, we won!" I jumped into his embrace. He then pulled away to look at my face, and his delicate fingers brushed my hair out of my face.

"You said my name correctly, Jay."

"And you said mine."

"Now how about that date?"

I smiled and raced him out of the doors. "I *will* be back boys." *It felt good to give my brother's reassurance for once.*

We rode in his truck into the night and out to an empty field. As I looked up at the stars I spoke out. "I did it guys. I did it for you, I hope you got to see it all."

"Jayleen, who are you talking to?"

"You see those stars up there?"

He smiled and took my hand. "Yes?"

"It's *them.*"

"I miss them Jay."

"They'll always be there Ben. Watching over us, no matter where we are."

We got back to Club Nine and a small party was being thrown. Everyone was there. Gwen, Ben, David, Luther, Eddie, Sam, and Ellie. *My family.*

I guess my Dad was right, there's always a light in the darkness; you just have to look, and I think I've found my light.

Made in the USA
Coppell, TX
02 December 2021

66973294R00059